I0682474

CAITLIN MYERS

Beyond A World Apart

First published by CEM Publishing LLC 2024

Copyright © 2024 by Caitlin Myers

First edition

ISBN: 979-8-218-47818-6

This book was professionally typeset on Reedsy.
Find out more at reedsy.com

To my mother and Elizabeth,
Thank you for believing in me.

"Not much chance for survival
If the Neon Bible is true"

-ARCADE FIRE, NEON BIBLE

Acknowledgement

I would like to thank and acknowledge my editor Elizabeth DeNoma and my unofficial book consultants Liz Hedgecock, Casey Dawes, and George J. Brown. Without you, this book would not have been possible. I am truly grateful. I would also like to acknowledge my inspiration for this novel, the *Eldorado, Everything the Nazi's Hate* documentary that sparked a deep dive into this period of history.

I

Part One

Dublin, Ireland
1928

Chapter 1

Cara's heart pounded as she discovered what was hidden inside the Winter 1927 issue of *Vogue*: a miniature newspaper featuring a naked woman on the cover. She quickly realized this little newspaper, tucked inside the magazine, had nothing to do with *Vogue* itself. Startled, she slammed the magazine shut and glanced around the haberdashery, finding it empty. Hal, the owner, was in the back of the shop, sharpening his shears for the umpteenth time. Had he seen her come in? The only sound was the scraping and grinding of metal. Cara cautiously peeked beneath the magazine cover again, revealing the little newspaper titled *Die Freundin*. Red blotches spread across her cheeks as she stared at the confident nude woman with wild curly hair, much like her own, and large, round breasts adorned with a long, beaded necklace. She slipped the newspaper out of the magazine and hid it inside her wool coat just as Hal emerged, his thick glasses perched on the edge of his bulbous nose.

"Thought it was you sneaking around the shop. Has the couture caught your eye again? Afraid those styles have not quite hit Henrietta Street, my dear," he said as he twirled his shears on his index finger.

He leaned his left elbow on a rickety wooden counter; behind

3

him, shelves were haphazardly stacked on top of one another, filled with fabrics of every color and texture imaginable. The glass display below him held shiny beads, appliques, and new sewing kit sets. Although business in Dublin was slow, Hal spent every day wiping the glass display clean and found creative ways to present fabrics that had not sold well. Some of the porous fabrics clung to the moisture of the rainy climate, but that distinct smell had become a comfort for Cara. She spent as much time as she could away from her crowded flat, and Hal's was like her real home: a place to dream and plan her escape.

"One day, I will leave Henrietta Street behind. I want to be a designer and make only the fanciest clothes. I need to find inspiration somewhere," she said.

"Remember us plebeians when you are too good to step foot in your home country again," Hal said, chuckling.

"I'll write to you," she retorted, "speaking of writing… any news?"

Hal sighed and put down his shears on the glass display, making a pretty clinking sound. He reached into his breast pocket to pull out an envelope and shake it in the air.

Cara ran up to Hal, threw her arms around his rotund belly, and squeezed. "Ronan!" she squealed.

"Ronan!" He mimicked in a high-pitched voice, "I'm starting to think you only come into my shop because I am a messenger between you and your exiled brother."

She snatched the letter out of his hands and thumbed over the lettering, a smile tugging at the corners of her mouth. She could recognize that handwriting anywhere.

"I will have you know that I also come into this haberdashery to pester you about petticoat mending and peruse last season's issues of *Vogue*," she said. She remembered the newspaper in her pocket, and her cheeks flushed bright red.

"Oh, dear. More petticoat orders? I'll grab your favorite plain white thread," he teased, "do you need extra fabric?"

Hal turned around to gather supplies around the shop, the harsh overhead lights reflecting off a shiny bald patch on his head. The rest of his hair was silvery gray. He tried his best to comb it over the patches.

"Yes, poor Mrs. Donnahue is pregnant again," Cara said, sighing with slumped shoulders.

If there was anything certain in this world, it was that Cara O'Shea was sick of mending petticoats. It was a task she found both monotonous and unfulfilling. Unfortunately for her, it was a task that she performed swiftly and notably well, creating buzz around her block of flats so that she could mend petticoats on the same day and at an affordable price. For mothers who were bursting at the seams with children, it was a small luxury they were willing to pay for. Cara saved the money from her mending requests and begged the mothers to give her other garments besides petticoats. Alas, despite it being 1928, most Dublin women seemed content to wear the same clothes despite the changing fashion trends, and so petticoat mending became Cara's specialty.

When she had the time and money, she loved to create her own designs: measuring and drawing out patterns on large sheets of paper, touching all the new fabrics at Hal's and carefully selecting the one she wanted the most, borrowing Hal's fabric shears to cut out the pattern, and eventually (and painstakingly) hand sewing every piece together. It had been a month since she completed her last project, a black and white A-line dress with pleats that started below the hip and made her figure look like one long straight line. A dress that Gran said looked like a potato sack with holes despite being in *Vogue*. Deflated, Cara had stuffed it in the back of her closet, along with her other creations that her Gran didn't seem to understand.

As she waited for Hal to gather plain white thread and to cut her scratchy undyed cotton cloth from the bolt, she stuffed her second piece of contraband, a letter from her brother she was forbidden to speak with, in her breast pocket. It felt heavy next to the newspaper despite both being on feather-light paper. She opened the Winter issue again and turned the pages to an image featuring women at a modeling school in Berlin. They wore what looked like men's oversized, striped suits and matching trousers. The women also wore collared button-up shirts—a fire lit inside her. Women wearing men's clothes?

Hal came out with the materials and began to ring them up. "Oh, my dearest Cara. I know that face. What have you found?"

"Have you seen this?" she asked excitedly. "Women are wearing men's clothing in Berlin. Look at these suits!" She turned the magazine over to show him the photo.

"That is risqué," he said, "you aren't thinking about making a suit, are you?"

Cara's eyes lit up the way they did only when she had an idea for a new project. "This could be the thing that gets me out of here! I could make and wear a suit and bring this fashion to Dublin. Maybe I could wear this to a big event where Ireland's wealthiest people will be, and they'll want me to make their clothes!"

"Cara, that doesn't make a lick of sense. Don't be dreaming; you are seventeen. Who is going to invite you to a high society event? Also, it's just a suit. The only difference is that some

6

women are wearing them. Women's suits do exist, but with skirts," Hal replied.

Cara pouted. "Please, Hal?" she pleaded. "Help me make it?"

Hal sighed. "Fine. Don't come crying to me when your Gran smacks you silly for being queer."

It wasn't the first time Hal had said this to her, but the fire inside of her raged on all the same.

With the daylight fading and fresh supplies in hand, Cara headed home to diligently work through the petticoat orders in her family's one-room flat. When she arrived, she quickly shoved her wool coat between a few failed sewing projects in the closet so her little sister, Maggie, would not be tempted to rifle through her pockets. However, to her surprise, only Gran was home, dozed off in a rocking chair with knitting on her lap. Her mother must have taken both her sisters to play with a family across the hall, and in this rare moment alone, Cara appreciated the semi-silence. The only sound that could be heard was the rhythmic breathing of Gran's deep sleep.

Cara flushed, realizing she was the only conscious one in the room. Could she read the letter and newspaper carefully, with Gran being none the wiser? If it was even a thought, she squashed it. She was sure the rest of the family would come busting through the doors and that the ever-curious Maggie would grab whatever was in her hands. There was no private space. Even the baths down the hall were communal. So, she set to work, remembering that at the end of this batch of mending, she could go to Hal's after school the next day to start her newest project. The letter and newspaper would have to wait for her secret hiding place with Molly, her best friend.

The soft light of dusk illuminated her workspace as she carefully mended rips and tears in each project and added

7

gussets for the pregnant Mrs. Donnahue. Her skilled hands moved swiftly and methodically, stitching each piece with precision and care. As she finished each order, she hung them over the baby's empty crib, her shining brown ringlet curls bouncing with every movement. When she thought she wouldn't finish before suppertime, Cara cut the last bit of thread with her teeth and rushed door to door within the block of flats to drop off the orders and collect her pay.

Chapter 2

To keep up appearances, Cara pretended to have the fear of God in her. On the surface, at least to the adults surrounding her, she was doing excellent work despite it being a great effort for her to appease the nuns, priests, teachers, Mom, and Gran. For example, at her school, she never had any uniform dress violations, was always on time for her classes, received decent marks, obeyed all her teachers, was chair of her community service club, and won a bronze medal for Leadership in Piety that had prayer hands engraved on it. This impressed Sister Agnes who had spoken with her family about the possibility of Cara joining their convent when she turned eighteen. If Cara ever felt that she'd stepped out of line, she immediately found time to go to confession. On the surface, she was a good Catholic, living her faith.

In reality, she would meet with Molly after school to open Ronan's letter and look at naked girls together.

She walked out of St. Kevin's and toward the church of the same name, a white stone building in constant battle with the moss and ivy. Spires pointed high toward the heavens, the tallest spire adorned with a crucifix. The opening was a stone archway, and a small statue of St. Kevin holding a rosary was tucked in on top. Cara's black t-strap heels clicked through the church's pathway, past the cemetery, and into the warmth of the vestibule. The winds were harsh, fighting her as she closed the church door and whistled through the walls' cracks. She sniffled and wiped her eyes, the sting of the cold weather lingering.

Next to her was a decorated bowl of holy water. She dipped her hand inside the oily water and made the sign of the cross. She then peeled off her wool coat to reveal her bright, white lace shawl that she only wore for church, took out her matching lace prayer cap from the coat pocket, and placed it on her head. The little sunlight that peeked through the clouds illuminated the stained-glass windows, brightening the colored glass and revealing Jesus at various stations of the cross. The church had high-vaulted ceilings with large, curved beams, a magnificent organ pipe, and gold-plated statues and crucifixes. Her favorite was a weeping statue of Mary, her shroud tightly hugging every curve of her body with a half-naked dead Jesus on her lap.

Taking a deep breath, Cara walked toward the back of the church and approached a confessional. Confessing something to a best friend was nerve-wracking enough, let alone to an adult man. Although confessions were supposed to be private, her heart beat against her chest as she opened the thin, lacquered wooden door and slipped inside the booth. It didn't matter how often she went; confession never got any easier. She sang an awkward hello, hung her shawl on the brass hook, and pulled down the kneeler. The priest on the other side of the confessional was behind a screen, but Cara knew it was Father Patrick from the outline and deep tone of his hello. She blew out a sigh of relief.

"Forgive me, Father, for I have sinned. It has been a week since my last confession," she recited.

"Go on, my child," Father Patrick said.

Cara took a breath to begin. "I cursed in front of my Gran. I ate my sister Maggie's chocolate and lied when she asked if I had taken it. And I received a letter from my brother, even though my family forbids me to communicate with him."

"Well, the first two confessions, Cara... oh rubbish," he said, "let's pretend I didn't say your name. This is an anonymous meeting with God."

Cara laughed. Father Patrick always found ways to remind his parish that he was human, just like them.

"I was hoping it was you today," she admitted, smiling.

"And here I am. Don't tell my big boss if it's okay with you." Behind the screen, he pointed toward the heavens and said, "Let's have a casual conversation. I'm sure it will result in a few Hail Marys and Our Fathers. We'll get there all the same. Except for the chocolate stealing. I am afraid you will need to make amends by replacing your sister's chocolate, and maybe on the way to make those amends, you can drop some off at the rectory."

"I will see what I can do, Father," she chuckled.

"The only thing better would be your apple cake. It wouldn't win many points with God, but I can promise that Sister Agnes and I would be quite pleased. We may show up at your family's door again, begging for you to be at the convent. Although, on second thought, we would likely chain your ankle to the oven and force you to make apple cake for the rest of your days," he said jokingly.

"It doesn't sound like the worst existence, baking for the rest of my days. I'm sure my customers wouldn't be too pleased that I've gone into baking and stopped mending. May I stop kneeling?" Her knees had fully deflated the upholstery in the kneeler, and her feet began to numb.

"No, you may not," Father Patrick responded. "I'm only joking. I do enjoy teasing the youth of this parish. Please, sit on the most comfortable sliver of wood behind you."

As Cara lifted the kneeler back into its position, she felt the blood rush back into her feet.

"Now, your brother. I know you love him dearly, but he lives in sin. Our association with him is also one of sin until he is ready to confess and start anew. We must love him and encourage him to be on the righteous path," Father Patrick continued.

Cara pulled at the loose stitching on her shawl, undoing a few knits. In her coat were the forbidden items she confessed to and the others she would never be able to.

"I don't understand why he ran away," Cara confessed, "nor why I am forbidden to speak with him. One day he was here, and the next he was gone. If I could understand my family's decision more, perhaps I would be more inclined to obey their wishes."

Cara observed Father Patrick's obscured figure scratching his chin, his gaze forward, lost in thought. They were silent for a moment, and all that could be heard was the creaking wood as she shifted on the hard bench. Her hamstrings were now going numb from the sharp circulatory cutoff. She scooted more toward the edge, knowing that it meant her bottom would be going numb next.

Father Patrick broke the silence. "I am not sworn to secrecy, and I believe you are old enough to know the truth."

He then shifted in his seat before confessing her own family's secret to Cara.

Chapter 3

"Oof!"

A flurry of garments and books spilled onto the cobblestones outside St. Kevin's.

Taking giant strides away from the confessionals, Cara had looked over her shoulder to ensure Father Patrick was not following her. Before she knew it, she'd collided with someone, her bottom on the cold, wet stone.

"I'm so sorry, I didn't—" Cara started. "Oh, it's you."

"It *is* me," Molly replied, helping Cara up. "You look like you've seen a ghost. Are you okay?"

"I'm fine. Confused? Can you still meet today?" Cara asked in one rushed breath.

"Yes, of course."

Cara helped Molly pick up the dropped items. Molly's otherwise straight strawberry blonde hair had one slight tendril curl framing her cheek. Her freckles hadn't come out yet, but in the summertime, her face would be a solar system of them. She was wearing a coat that Cara had made for her one year for Christmas that flared at the hips. Cara even embroidered Molly's initials on the breast of the coat, followed by a small flower. It had taken her months, so she swelled with pride whenever she saw Molly wearing it. It hugged her figure

13

perfectly while being modest and fashionable.

Cara curled her lip into a smile, picked up the slight tendril curl, and let it go gently.

"One curl, Cara! Just one!" Molly exclaimed and held out her white-gloved index finger.

"Be grateful it's only one!" Cara said, picking up her section of thick curly hair and bouncing it up and down.

They giggled together, and warmth washed over Cara, affording her relief.

"I have to drop this off first," Molly held up a donation envelope. "But I will meet you there, okay?"

Cara nodded and headed toward their secret spot, the back entrance of St. Kevin's bell tower. The bell tower was accessed daily for afternoon mass, but at all other times, it was devoid of people. Molly, always more rebellious, had grabbed a spare key while completing some filing for the church office after school one day. Since then, the bell tower had become their meeting place, where they would sit under the stairwell and share secrets, dreams, and fears. It was here that they pushed boundaries of being good, obedient girls. Molly frequently took communion wine from the cupboards of the church's tabernacle and brought it to the bell tower for them to consume. It wasn't consecrated yet, so technically, it was not the blood of Jesus.

The wind and rain blew in gusts against Cara's body as she approached the bell tower. The walk was only a few minutes, but it took twice as long, fighting against the pelting droplets. All she saw were her feet as the wind began to open her eyes.

The only reassurance she had was in her pocket. The newspaper and the envelope wore down softly with every touch of her clammy hands. She was constantly checking

14

to ensure they were still there, that they hadn't somehow disappeared from the last time she checked. She finally reached the bell tower and hid underneath its arch until she saw Molly emerge, waving a jug of wine victoriously, her eyes squinting from the wind.

Molly pushed the key into the back of the bell tower door and slipped inside. Cara stood watch momentarily, glancing around to ensure no one saw them, and followed.

They sat side by side on the thin, wrought iron staircase as Molly uncorked the wine with the Codd bottle opener she stole from her parents. They each took long swigs, the flush warming them from the inside. Their cheeks were round and rosy, flushing more with each sip.

"Your lips, Molly. They're so purple!" Cara exclaimed, catching a giggle in her throat.

Molly looked down and giggled into her chest. She came back up, and her sparkling eyes gazed into Cara's. "Get it off for me then," she said.

She stretched her neck out, and Cara attempted to wipe off the purple with her thumb.

"It's not coming off," Cara smiled.

"Your teeth are purple!" Molly said with a laugh. "We're going to get caught!"

"Shh!" Cara put her index finger on Molly's lips. This made Molly laugh even louder.

They settled down and caught their breath until Cara began to hiccup, spinning them into a whirl of laughter again. Cara was now laughing and hiccupping, attempting various unsuccessful methods of resetting her diaphragm until they finally stopped from no particular method, and she could breathe normally again.

"You're such a drunk," Molly gently patted her on the arm.

"I take after all the legends in my family," Cara said, bowing slightly as Molly clapped.

"Bravo! Encore!"

"No encore, I do not want more hiccups!" Cara said.

"But you're so adorable when you hiccup," Molly said. She noticed Cara blush and nudged her.

Cara nudged her back, and Molly slipped her arm through Cara's, placing her head on Cara's shoulder.

"What did you have to talk to me about?" Molly asked. "You looked awful coming out of confession."

She began gently rubbing Cara's arm. Molly did this frequently. Cara saw other girls in her class behaving this way, like how they would link arms or rest their heads on their friends' laps. The only difference was Cara didn't think they felt so ashamed. So why did she feel guilty when Molly touched her in this way? Cara unhooked their arms, pulled out the newspaper and envelope from her breast pocket, and presented them to Molly.

"Another letter from Ronan and... what is this? Oh my," she said, looking at the naked woman. "Surely you didn't tell Father about this," Molly's eyebrows were drawn together.

"Of course, I didn't tell him," Cara said. "I found it hidden in Hal's latest issue of *Vogue*. I don't know what the title means. I think it's in German."

Molly's eyes widened as she flipped through the newspaper pages while Cara looked over her shoulder.

"Here's the plan," Molly said, looking up at her, "you read Ronan's letter out loud while I look at this for a moment. I need to inspect it thoroughly."

"There is no way I am reading something else while you are

looking at nudey ladies."

Molly ignored Cara and turned to the next page, which contained what looked like a poem and a few advertisements. Molly attempted to read the German words dramatically, waving her arms up and down like she was talking to an audience, looking silly overall. Cara knew that she was impersonating her mother, Catherine, a former stage actress, who she had observed performing monologues when she became fuddled. However, it all sounded like mumbled consonants, but the histrionic performance made Cara giggle. Ultimately, the girls could not be entirely sure of the newspaper's written contents, as neither understood German.

The newspaper had a letterhead, table of contents, and excerpts on the front page. Inside, there were long, scrolling articles and even the occasional cartoon. They would only pause and admire what they could understand, which were the women photographed, and not all were nude. Some were posing together outside wearing trousers and suit coats, some were photographed at a club with drinks in front of them on a white linen table, and some looked like men who dressed as women.

The girls lingered the longest on photographs of the nude women. Their breasts were out on display, and one image showed a woman touching herself.

Cara felt the moisture between her legs as she saw the pictures. "I think I've peed myself," she whispered.

"Why are you whispering? The nudey ladies can't hear you, Cara," Molly giggled. She turned another page; front and center were two women kissing.

"Girls can't kiss girls!" Cara exclaimed.

"Well, obviously they can," Molly said, pointing at the photo.

"Maybe the German women are so desperate for men after the war that they have had to resort to kissing each other."

Cara crossed her arms indignantly and shook her head. "I would never kiss a girl."

"I think I would. Kissing boys is boring. Their lips are always chapped, and their breath smells," Molly said. She turned to the final page to find a closing paragraph.

Cara cleared her throat and stood up from the iron staircase. She held out her hand for Molly to deposit the newspaper. Molly pouted her lips, and Cara wanted nothing more in that moment than to find out how soft they were.

"Can I keep it? I promise to hide it somewhere," Molly said.

"Molly, it's mine. I found it. I think it's perverting you," Cara said, grabbing the newspaper to put back in her coat pocket.

"Look me in the eyes and tell me you wouldn't kiss me." Molly's round, red lips parted slightly, tempting Cara.

Molly got up from the staircase and gently pushed Cara against the cold stone wall. Cara's heart raced inside her chest, her breathing growing shallower as Molly's face closed on hers. Cara closed her eyes, but no kiss came. Molly backed away.

"Caught you. You are perverted, just like I thought," Molly said, smiling.

Cara's cheeks burned, and her ears tinged with pink. "You're the one who came up to me."

Molly sat back down on the staircase. "I was testing to see if you were a funny little fairy. And I think you are."

"So are you!" Cara retorted.

"I can be a funny fairy sometimes. At least I've had some boyfriends. It all evens out," Molly reasoned. She sat back down on the staircase.

Cara couldn't argue with that. No matter how many boys

asked her out, she always found an excuse to turn them down.

She thought it best to change the subject rather than fixate on the strangeness that had occurred. "I don't want to talk about it anymore. Let's read Ronan's letter."

She pulled the letter out of her pocket, cleared her throat, and began.

Dear Cara,

I miss you and the family with all my heart. I hope you don't mind that I had Hal place something in your favorite magazine, a little treat from Berlin. Berlin is astounding and strange and everything I could have ever hoped for. I dream you can visit me someday and see how happy I am here. Maybe you could discover some new things about yourself too. I do not condone running away from your problems, but sometimes, a little distance does help clear the mind. There is so much I want to teach you about a new world that will, hopefully, one day reach Dublin. However, I also understand that not only the family but also the culture tends to be stuck in their ways. You and I are not much different from each other. I'm sending you a ticket to Hal's that you can use whenever you visit me in Berlin. Choose a date, and I would be more than happy to host you.

All my love,
Ronan

Chapter 4

The girls parted ways from the bell tower at St. Kevin's and headed back to their homes. Cara's heels clicked on the wet, reflective cobblestone road, the sound growing quick and frantic as if she hoped she could run away from the secrets of the past few days.

Gray clouds rolled in overhead and threatened to stay. At least Cara had seen the sun earlier if only for a moment, peeking out as she had walked into the church for confession.

She turned right onto Henrietta Street and came across the rail line that separated the road in two. She carefully placed a foot on the edge of one of the rails, then another, and walked it as a tightrope. Why did Charlie Chaplin need a long stick to hold to walk a tightrope? Cara could walk the rail line with her arms tightly at her sides. Then, one of her feet slipped off a wet portion of the rail, and she nearly toppled over, just managing to land with both feet solid on the even ground. Shaken by the almost accident, she walked on the safety of the solid street until she arrived at her block of flats.

The flat she lived in was originally a single-family home converted into multiple living quarters, with different families occupying each room.

Climbing up the stairs was challenging, as specific steps

had holes in the rotted-out wood. This required her to dance around those tender areas, fearing she could break the wood in half. Lanterns lit the hallway dimly, and it smelled of mildew and dirty nappies. The runner, once a vibrant blue and white, was muddied gray from multiple winters of soggy shoes and the dried drips of wet brollies. Her family was lucky enough to have their galley kitchen, but they did share a toilet with three other families, which made for eighteen people to one toilet and one bath. Conveniently, their family's flat contained three chamber pots in the likely event that the toilet was occupied.

Cara discovered she was not well off when required to go to a classmate's birthday party. She exclaimed to her classmates how incredible it was to have multiple toilets and a room for each family member. Not a single chamber pot occupied that house. What luxury!

When Cara arrived home, the block's noise was deafening. Children were screaming, and a few babies were crying, creating a cacophony of high-pitched suffering. She passed by a room with the door slightly ajar to hear a woman shouting at her husband, resulting in a loud slap, thump, and, eventually, a female groan.

Cara walked faster and slipped quietly into her family's flat. The noise of the hallway muffled behind her as she shut the door.

Gran was in her favorite armchair; head bowed, knitting slumped in her hands, catching snores in her throat. Cara's mum, Ana, was on the bed, her back facing the door as she and the baby napped together. Her little sister Maggie lay in the far corner of their shared bed, clutching a stuffed bear.

With the room sleeping peacefully among the muffled chaos of the block, Cara decided to follow suit. She removed her shoes and then her coat, gently placing them on the hook and shoving them in the back of her closet. She climbed on top of her bed. It only took her a few moments to doze off to a strange place.

They held hands and ran out of the chapel into the warm spring air. They went to a park and rolled around in the grass, laughing and watching the clouds in the sky above them spin. While they were lying flat on the grass, Molly rolled over to Cara and put her head on Cara's chest.

Molly's hair was an ethereal, glowing, shiny strawberry blond. Her skin was soft and smooth, and she smelled like roses. Whenever they touched, Cara would stumble over her words. Molly's freckles came out fiercely in the summertime, and Cara could spend an afternoon counting every new one on her face.

"I wish we could lay like this forever," Molly said.

Cara's stomach flooded with butterflies. She put her arm on Molly's back and gently rubbed it as she had seen in the romantic silent films.

Molly hovered above her and then kissed her deeply. Cara kept her eyes open for a moment out of shock, then closed them, kissing Molly back fiercely. After a few seconds, they pulled apart, and Molly laid her head back on Cara's chest. Cara watched her head rise and fall, and they lay like that in the height of the afternoon sun.

Before sunset, they walked together, hand-in-hand, new dots sprouting on their noses and arms. As they approached Molly's, she looked at Cara, twirling a handful of Cara's hair with a smile.

Suddenly, the image of Molly and the sunny day morphed. Cara was sitting on the floor of her room on a circular plaited rug with a petticoat on her lap. She was going in and out with a needle and thread, the memory of their time together fueling the monotony

22

of mending the garment. She kept stabbing herself but didn't feel the punctures in her calloused fingertips. As she got into a rhythm, the needle slipped through the fabric too swiftly, and she jabbed her pointer finger all the way through, the needle sticking clear through the nail bed. Immediately, blood started pouring out onto the petticoat. The once-white cotton cloth bloomed with thick red liquid.

Ana came through the front door with the baby on her hip. As her mother looked at her on the floor, a petticoat soaked in blood, she screamed, "What have you done?"

* * *

It took Cara almost a month to make her suit. She took no other orders at the time, working day in and day out to make sure all the obvious stitches were hidden and that she had measured every piece correctly. The hem of the trousers fit just right, and she even had to add a zipper, an unfamiliar element.

Hal had patiently answered her questions and discounted some of the fabric if she promised to help him with his annual end-of-winter sale at the haberdashery.

Although her entire family may have lived in one large room, they never bothered to ask her questions about what she was making, complaining only that she woke before the sun to work by candlelight. It was tricky, but she got the hang of it after a few stitch tear-outs. She added padding in the shoulders and borrowed her father's button-up shirt.

Finally, her suit was finished.

Cara tried it on. She pranced around the room with her chest puffed out and did a silly dance in front of Maggie. She shoved her hands inside the deep pockets of the trousers and continued to prance about the room, a gleam in her eye. Her sister clapped and demanded an encore from the dancing Cara until Gran took hold of her shoulders and shook her back into reality.

Cara thought she was joking at first—a little playful jolt. Gran was serious.

"I knew you were just like your perverted brother, mixing up girl things and boy things. You are not rich enough to be a Lady of Llangollen, girl," Gran said.

"What is a Lady of Llangollen?" Cara asked, her brows furrowed.

Gran shoved her in frustration, and Cara tripped over the bottom of her trousers, ripping them at the hem. She caught a few splinters on the bottom of her feet from the unpolished wood floor as she fell.

"What is going on?" Ana asked upon entering the flat, having just changed a very heavy and messy nappy in the flat's shared toilets. She looked down at Cara on the ground, noticing her torn trousers.

"Dear god, what is this costume?" Ana snorted with laughter. "Are you joining the ladyboys of Dublin? Giving us a show?"

"No wonder she's never had any interest in dating. She'd rather be a boy than date one! You are too poor to be a Llangollen girl!" Gran shouted yet again.

"Oh, she is not pretending to be a Lady of Llangollen, Ma. Calm down. It's just a costume," Ana said.

Finally, Cara spoke. "This is the next upcoming fashion trend: women in men's clothing. I saw it in *Vogue*! I want to be a designer. I want to design what the socialites are wearing. I know I can do it!"

"Wait until Father McKinny hears about this," Gran spat.

Father McKinny was known for being the harshest at St. Kevin's parish.

"You'll forget by the morning, you old bat," Cara muttered through sniffles. She got herself up and stomped off toward the toilet.

"Don't talk to your Gran that way!" Ana shouted after her. "You owe her an apology, Cara Anne!"

Cara was already undressed and painstakingly removing the splinters from her foot, vigilantly watching the toilet door in the mirror. It was difficult for Cara to turn off the tears once they started, so she wept as she picked out the wood embedded in her pale skin.

She was unsure whether Gran had meant for her to be pushed down or if maybe she lost her balance.

Cara was only ever spanked a few times as a small child. Once, Cara had broken Gran's treasured porcelain dog statue, a life-size Dalmatian with a blue collar and human eyes. A marble had flown out of her hand and clipped off the edge of the dog's ear, and Gran had become so enraged she beat Cara's bottom nearly raw. Cara had only been five years old. Since then, she had tried to stay out of Gran's way. They mainly got along, and Gran occasionally became affectionate toward her.

Tonight's display was the most significant reaction Gran's ever had to anything Cara made.

Cara skipped supper, telling her mother she wasn't hungry, and she sat cross-legged on her bed, back facing the rest of the room, mending what had torn so she could show Molly at church in the morning. The tears had dried, leaving her eyes puffy and bloodshot. However, she was focused on each stitch, ensuring every snag was tapered and the lines were clean. That was until Maggie plopped on her bed, grabbed her hair,

25

and yanked her head back, calling her a strange fairy. Cara shooed her away and continued to stitch, each one precise and meticulous. Maggie informed her it would be much easier to use a sewing machine than to hand-sew everything.

"Thanks so much for that, Maggie. I had no idea. I'll go get one from a factory." Cara rolled her eyes.

Maggie curled up to Cara and whispered, "Gran said you are acting this way on purpose. That you've been hurting her more ever since Da died. What did she mean by that?"

"This isn't about Da. I don't know. She's halfway in the grave, Maggie. She's senile, you know?" Cara whispered back.

In the corner, Maggie popped up on her bed and laid her head on the pillow. "What is a Lady of Llangollen?"

"Your guess is as good as mine. Stop asking me questions; you're acting the maggot."

"I want to go to sleep soon," Maggie said with tired eyes.

Ana approached them with the baby on her hip, placing her in the crib beside the bed. "Finish up in the morning, Cara. You have a big day tomorrow. More petticoat orders."

Cara audibly sighed and dramatically threw her needle, thread, and trousers to the side. She peeled back the quilt to slip her legs underneath, grabbed a stuffed bear Molly had given her for her birthday, and propped it up on her pillow. She squeezed it tightly and stroked its fuzzy head, putting her nose deep into it. If she inhaled deeply enough, she could smell Molly's scent of talcum powder and rose perfume that she stole from her mother. It brought her comfort to sleep with every night. She closed her eyes.

Chapter 5

As the late winter chill thawed into an unseasonably warm spring, so too did the ice thaw in the O'Shea household. April skipped over rain showers, and the gray clouds that seemed a permanent fixture in Irish winters dissipated, giving way to a pale blue sky. After what felt like a harsh punishment by piles of petticoats, Cara was finally allowed outside to enjoy the sunshine.

She met up with Molly beyond Henrietta Street in favor of Dublin's public parks. Some of the winter rains left the parks seemingly irredeemable, with pothole puddles and thick, wet mud cakes among drowning blades of grass. They walked the cleared paths together, jumping over any threats to their dry clothing. However, as the sun continued to shine, they saw new emerald swards in the dirt, and the warmed earth became a welcoming cushion for an outdoor luncheon.

Molly had recently stopped stealing the unconsecrated communion wine and brought a hip flask filled with whiskey from her mother's supply. She wore a long brown skirt and button-down blouse with custom-sewn eyelets at her puffed capped short sleeves, a brown belt that cinched her waist, and a light cardigan. Cara wore a bright yellow calf-length floral dress, fitted at the bodice, that flowed outward at the hip, giving her a stunning hourglass figure. Cara made both outfits from a collection of fabric scraps and donated garments.

They took turns taking swigs out of the hip flask, their backs resting against a towering oak tree. Although Cara and Molly had only seen each other in church and school, their discernible tension had grown. Molly took off her cardigan, revealing soft, supple skin. She pushed back her hair to reveal her long crane neck and gazed at the warm sun, her face glowing in its light. She lazily unbuttoned a few buttons of her blouse, revealing a camisole placed low on her chest, showing off her cleavage.

Cara never initiated skin contact with Molly, fearing that she and her family might be right about her being strange. As she suspected, the proof was in replaying that day in the bell tower over in her head when Molly almost kissed her. She fancied that Molly's kiss creeping into her dreams further proved her strangeness.

Cara adjusted her position and tightly folded her arms around her knees, her yellow dress pulled across her lap. She chewed on her cheek, saliva flooding her mouth.

After a conversation with her mother during what seemed like a never-ending era of punishment, she discovered that the Ladies of Llangollen were two socialite women from separate families who moved out of Ireland to live with one another in Wales. They wanted to escape the familial pressures they felt to marry men, so they ran away together to settle in the countryside.

Her mother had described the rumored intimate relationship between the women and how they dressed in trousers and top hats. Cara understood because it seemed that her choices were either the convent or marriage and the family was losing faith that she'd ever seek out marriage.

Ronan's travel arrangements were looking better every day, but she had not written to him since his last letter.

Molly tapped her on the shoulder, bringing her out of her thoughts.

"Where did you go?" she asked softly.

"Far away from here," Cara said despondently.

Molly's freckles were fiercely on display, the pink tinge underneath highlighting her strong cheekbones. Cara's heart pounded against her chest, their faces centimeters apart like they were back at the bell tower.

Molly's breath was strong with peated whiskey. It was almost too much for Cara to bear. She closed her eyes and turned her head away from Molly. Molly stroked Cara's arm, lightly tracing her fingers on sun-kissed skin. She put her head on Cara's shoulder, and Cara stiffened at the weight of it.

As the sun warmed their bodies, Cara couldn't ignore the electric current that surged between them – a forbidden desire that had been simmering within her for years. Molly's delicate fingers traced patterns on Cara's arm, sending shivers down her spine and making her heart race. The world around them faded away as Molly's fingers moved higher, brushing against the bare skin of Cara's neck. Her breath hitched as Molly's touch grew bolder, tracing the curve of her jawline. With a fierce determination, she turned towards Molly and met her gaze with an intensity that left no room for doubt. Their lips met in a hesitant, electrifying kiss.

Cara pulled away first.

"We can't do this. I'm so confused," she said in a low voice.

"Why not?" Molly asked.

Cara sighed. "The day I came out of confession, and we went to the bell tower, Father Patrick told me something about

29

Ronan."

"Well, what did he say?" Molly asked.

"He said that Ronan was caught kissing another boy, and he gave Ronan a choice to defeat his ungodly sins, to either start his pastoral studies or find a girl to marry. I'm afraid I've caught this disease. I'm afraid I—"

"Oh, Cara. You *are* a strange fairy. What will your family think? Having two in the family?" Molly teased.

Cara's face flushed red.

"I'm only joking," Molly commented, nudging Cara.

Cara looked down at her hands. "I'm attempting to have a serious conversation with you."

"Okay, you may go on," Molly said, rolling her eyes.

"I am a good person. I get good grades, go to church and confess, and follow the rules. Why can I not defeat this?" Cara asked seriously.

"Cara," Molly sighed, "why do you follow some rules, like going to confession, but not others, like making men's clothing for yourself?"

"I'll have to be a complete rule follower from now on. Gran and Ma have been suspicious since I made the suit," Cara said.

"Imagine what would happen if they found the nudey book," Molly said.

Cara turned to her with a stern expression on her face.

"Or Ronan's letter."

They sat on the grass and listened to the wind blow through the trees.

"There's no one here," Molly observed, "and if we want to find out if you are, you know—strange—we may as well make sure."

Cara thought about this momentarily and felt a pang of

30

shame in her stomach. "I already know," she said, picking a blade of grass from underneath her feet and peeling it in strips.

"For sure?" Molly asked.

Cara nodded. "Maybe I could run away. Live with Ronan for a bit. I do have his ticket."

"You're only seventeen," Molly reasoned. "Besides, the only reason Ronan ran away was because he was found bent over with Father Patrick's dingle inside his behind," Molly said.

"That's not what–"

"Not what Father Patrick said? So now he's covering his arse," Molly said.

"How did you find out?" Cara asked.

"Mum's got a drunken sieve for a mouth. She didn't even wake up this morning, can you believe that? Too hungover to get out of bed," she replied casually.

"What else did she say about it?" Cara asked.

"Well, Ronan came to her to tell her what had happened before leaving, and she told him to leave the country. She still has friends in the theater community in Berlin, and that's where he went. Nothing can be as scandalous as that," Molly reasoned, "not even kissing under an oak tree with no one around."

Cara shook her head, "I don't know. It feels good but so wrong at the same time."

"That's the best part," Molly whispered.

She leaned over and played with the buttons on Cara's dress. "I don't want to pressure you into something you don't want to do—"

Cara looked into Molly's bright blue eyes, letting them pierce through her. "You know that I want to. Especially with you," she admitted, her bottom lip slightly quivering.

31

The wind rustled the budding leaves on the oak tree. Blades of grass danced in the air's gentility—blue skies. Warm sun. Spring wind. Beautiful girl.

Cara wasn't perfect. If what Molly confessed about Father Patrick was true, what was the harm in a bit of kissing?

Molly gently pulled Cara's chin to hers, and Cara leaned in, kissing her softly and sweetly. Molly teased her tongue on Cara's lips, wanting to explore her.

Cara backed away once more. "We're still in public, Molly," she laughed nervously, rubbing the back of her neck. She whipped her head around, but there was nothing but a nature oasis and people far off the carved path, walking in the distance.

"I got excited. I'm sorry, we can go slower," Molly said, tucking a strand of curly hair behind Cara's ear. "No one is here, my strange little fairy."

Cara leaned in and finally let go. She was entranced, driven by years of suppressed desire toward her best friend. Letting go meant exploring roads long blocked off by large yellow danger signs. *Warning!* They would say, *High Voltage!* with a skull and crossbones.

As they kissed, Cara grew bolder, sliding her hand underneath Molly's camisole. She felt Molly's warm, bare breast in her hand, and without a thought, she started caressing her nipple. Molly caught a breath. Cara moaned, and Molly whispered to her, "More, please. More."

Cara released her nipple and kissed her way down to Molly's center, awkwardly sliding down her skirt and checking to ensure no one was watching them. She stroked her first with the light pressure of her tongue to see how she would react. Molly's back arched against the grass with every stroke, so Cara continued in different ways, with more pressure, less pressure, in circles, zigzags, fast, slow. Seeing how Molly reacted made her wet in between her legs.

"Something's happening," Molly said, "I might explode." Her body convulsed and twisted in a way that Cara had never seen before. She was breathless. "I've never felt that before," Molly admitted.

Molly hiked her skirt back up and pulled her cardigan over her shoulders. Cara wiped her mouth with her hand and smelled her breath.

"Let me have the whiskey," Cara demanded. Molly handed over the flask, and Cara drained it in seconds.

"Save some for the fishes, Cara!"

"I smell like your... well," Cara mumbled.

"Well, you were down there for a while. Did you enjoy it?" Molly smirked.

Cara moved closer to Molly and stroked the bottom of her lip with her tongue. Molly moved in to kiss her, but Cara backed away.

"We really should get home," Cara said, a pang of shame building in her gut.

Molly's eyes widened. "Sure," was all she managed to utter.

They packed their belongings and walked together; Molly's arm interlaced with Cara's. The uneven cobblestone roads stretched long before them. Reality started to set in as they approached Henrietta Street. They saw the beggars begging for their next meal, children running around in nothing but nappies or torn clothing, rubbish piles in nonsensical places, and the overall stench of poverty. They separated at Cara's large block, their fingers intertwined, lingering in the space between them.

Molly turned around to face Cara. "I feel something for you.

More than friends," she said, almost in a whisper. Her eyes began to well, and she cleared her throat before speaking again. "Are you ashamed of me?" She asked in a low voice.

The color drained from Cara's face as she looked blankly at Molly. "I'm ashamed of me. I know I am different, and I wish I could be normal. And now I've dragged you into this sickness, too!"

Molly wiped tears from her eyes. "What if we are not sick? What about what Ronan said about Berlin? Things are different there. We could go and be together."

Cara considered this for a moment before holding out her hand for Molly to take. "I love you," Cara admitted, "and I am so scared."

She watched Molly wipe tears from her eyes and walk away.

When she entered her one-room flat, Cara's mother stood there waiting for her, her hands folded across her chest, tears threatening to spill out of her eyes. Cara stopped at this sight, leaning away from Ana.

Gran was on her chair, thick glasses on the edge of her nose, looking down at Cara, not with disdain this time but with genuine concern.

Did someone see them? Had they found the letters?

34

Chapter 6

That sunny afternoon was forever tainted for Molly. Her mother, Catherine Byrnne, killed herself that beautiful spring day while she and Cara were at the park.

Ana, Cara's mother, had visited their home as she did every week, "for her goddamn sanity," to get away from her three children and spend time with a friend. She would frequently return from Catherine's, stumbling through their front door and tripping over the plaited rug despite it being in the exact location when she left. She would laugh at these missteps, her ruddy cheeks puffed out, and take the baby from Gran to feed her. "I'm about to overflow," she'd say before putting the baby on her tit.

That weekly ritual was cut short when no answer came after Ana casually rapped on the Byrnne's door, as she would any Wednesday. Then, as the seconds turned to minutes, she knocked again. When no answer came, she hit more furiously.

"I knew in my gut something wasn't right," she said while recounting the story. Hal lived next door and, in a strange coincidence, happened to be home and broke down Catherine's door. They found her hanging from the ceiling, rope taught, neck snapped, eyes bulging. A note lay beneath her feet.

The note detailed her love for her family and dedication to God. She explained that, as many times as she tried, she could not break her dependence on drink. She spoke about how negatively it affected her relationships, including the one with her daughter. Ana recounted that before the note, Catherine never mentioned she wanted to stop drinking.

As Molly's father made his way home after receiving the telegram, Ana convinced him to do more digging and order a complete examination of Catherine before she was interned. What they uncovered was the real reason she died. According to Ana, Catherine had no other choice.

When Catherine's belly eventually began to swell with life, the town would know the impossible timing of it all. Molly's father was away working for the season and had not been home in months. She would rather risk the mortal sin of suicide and directly pray for God's mercy than be alive another moment in the harsh whispers of the church's disgraces.

Molly's family held a funeral with a half-open casket to hide any lingering evidence potentially showing at her waist. It was another unseasonably warm day, and St. Kevin's Church seemed to trap the heat of the sun and the funeral attendees.

Cara's curls were plastered wet on her forehead, and her palms began to sweat as she approached the altar. She knelt at the casket, made the sign of the cross, and looked at Catherine's lifeless body.

The casket lining was a pale rose-pink silk, snagged in some places, with a few lingering balls of lint. Catherine wore a thick black wool dress with delicate lace detail that covered her neck to ankles. The dress was a sack on her petite frame, drowning her in the thick wool fabric. Nevertheless, whoever had done her makeup put the color back in her cheeks; she looked happier dead than she had alive.

Cara remembered Catherine at her happiest, coming home from a play. Catherine had wanted to spend her life on the stage but settled for attending the occasional show in Dublin. That night, she wore a beaded gown that she paid Cara to make, and when she got home, she poured herself a glass of whiskey, which she kept in a wedding-gifted glass carafe. The glass was hand-blown and covered in an intricate diamond pattern. She sat Molly and Cara down to tell them all about her night out, and without a filter, about her life before she had met Molly's Dad. She had known the actors on stage that night and felt nostalgic about her time at the theater, even telling them she had an opportunity to follow the troupe on a tour to London.

"Right around that time, I found out I was pregnant with you, Molly!" she exclaimed.

"You mean you weren't married yet, mum?" Molly's jaw dropped, and her innocent ten-year-old face brightened with surprise at the scandal.

Catherine giggled and held her finger to her lips. "A wee shotgun wedding. Don't tell anyone, girls. It's now our little secret."

The next day, after Cara had slept over, she eagerly went into the living room to hear more stories. However, when Catherine woke up, her wrinkled frown lines seemed to have burrowed deeper into her skin as she rattled a large pot on the metal stove to heat porridge for the kids. She took a deep breath and sighed before shakily pouring grain from a storage container, but the controlled breath turned into short gasping sobs that caught in her throat. Her most challenging acting role was her own life, escaping occasionally only to return to the big stage of reality.

Cara shook this memory from her mind and reached out for Catherine's hand. Despite a line of attendees behind her wanting to pay their respects, she took her time. She held Catherine's cold, fleshy fingers, bowed her head in prayer, and squeezed her eyes tight. Even if a prayer could reach the dead, what could she say that would remedy the situation? Still, Cara tried, and the low murmurs of the crowd began to fade away.

What awaits you is kinder and more loving than what you know on Earth, she repeated in her head. It was then that Cara saw Catherine's figure precipitate in her mind. Catherine wore a vacant expression, her hand clutching her chest, surrounded by endless space. She stared at Cara with a pained expression before vanishing as quickly as she appeared. Cara came to as an attendee tapped her shoulder, asking her to move, as the queue to say goodbye was getting long.

* * *

After the funeral, Cara found Molly outside smoking a cigarette, her back against the wall of the brick church. Cara had not spent time alone with Molly since her mother passed; their days were filled with family coming in and planning arrangements. Seeing her outside, her hair released from its tight bun, and her blonde hair glittering in the sunlight made Cara's heart flutter.

"Taking a break?" Cara asked.

"Splitting the stones. I'm sweating in there," Molly said, tapping the end of her cigarette.

Cara nodded and took the cigarette from Molly, putting it to her lips and inhaling deeply.

Molly caught a sob in her throat. "Cara," she cried, "What

am I going to do?"

Cara quickly put out the cigarette against the brick and pulled her friend into an embrace. She gently cupped Molly's face, kissed her on her cheeks and forehead, and embraced her again.

"You helped me when my Da passed," Cara said, "Now, I will help you."

They stayed like that for a while.

After the burial, Molly's dad suggested that she and Cara walk in the warm spring air to get some color on their cheeks. They walked and walked and walked, seemingly outside of Dublin, outside of Ireland, to their oasis. Long grass was growing on the side of a large hill, flowing in and out like seaweed caught in a gentle tide. The image was brilliantly similar to the day that Catherine died: the sky was a clear, vivid blue above them, and birds were singing. They decided to lie in the middle of a grassy knoll and stare at the clouds passing through the sky.

Molly placed her head on Cara's chest, rising and falling with each rhythmic breath. It was odd how something tragic could happen during a beautiful spring season, how the rest of nature continues its cycle without missing a beat. Molly peered up at Cara, looked over her, and placed her elbow on the soft grass. Cara smiled at her.

"You don't talk much about your Da," Molly remarked.

"Not much to talk about," Cara said.

"You always say that. What if I'm not like you? What if I want to talk about my mum?"

"Then you can talk about her. I'll listen. I put my nose in *Vogue* and focus on making patterns, mending, and designing because it helps distract me from my Da's death. It's hard to explain; it's like I go into a trance when I work with my hands. It must be genetic because Gran started to knit after she lost her son. Ronan started going to church more to process Da's death, but perhaps not in the way we had been thinking…" Cara trailed off.

Molly laughed at this realization.

"You may not be the same. Everyone grieves differently, Molly," Cara told her.

"I think we should run away from this mess," Molly said.

Cara stroked Molly's cheek with her thumb, and Molly sank into the touch.

"You must take care of your Da. He needs you," Cara said.

"Who will take care of me when he's away?" Molly asked.

"I will," Cara said.

"Promise you won't leave me," Molly said.

Cara leaned in and brushed her lips against Molly's. Cara then put her arm around Molly's shoulders as she sank into her chest. They held each other until the sun began to set, red, pink, orange, and golden hues peeking through the darkening clouds. They got themselves together and walked back to town.

Molly did not want to be alone the night she buried her mother, so she followed Cara up the stairs in her block of flats, hoping to stay over.

To their surprise, their families were waiting for them, making for a crowded entrance. Ana was pacing the room with the baby. Gran was rocking on her chair with such force that Cara thought she would fly out of it. Even Molly's father, Declan, though the girls rarely ever saw him, was awkwardly positioned with his arms folded across his chest. It was as if he was imagining what a disappointed father would look like and decided to put on his debut performance. They stared at each other, tension building with every beat of deafening quiet.

Cara broke the silence.

"A wee bit crowded for a single room," she laughed nervously.

"It's time to go home, Molly," Declan said.

Molly's eyes darted around the room and then to her father. "I was hoping to stay here. I am finding it difficult to be in the flat alone," Molly confessed.

"You are not alone. I'm there," Declan said indignantly. He was a large, muscular man with dark hair on his arms and a long, wiry beard. He wore a dark gray flat cap to cover his balding head.

"Yes, well. Perhaps we could make an exception if it is not too much of an inconvenience. Ana, you would not know I was here," Molly said.

When no one responded to Molly, Cara couldn't take the awkward silence any longer. "What is happening? Why is everyone acting so strange?" she asked, shaking her head and furrowing her brows in confusion.

Then, Gran broke the silence, unable to hold her tongue. "You little pervert," she spat at Cara.

"Gran!" Ana said, shocked.

"It's quite all right, Ma. I was waiting for that. Thank you, Gran," Cara replied, anger rising in her throat, "perhaps in your senility, you've forgotten that we've buried someone today. Molly's mother died, but yes, please tell me how I am a little pervert."

The adults glanced at each other, still wearing the black outfits from the funeral. The baby began to wail. Cara guessed she sensed the discomfort of the room. Frustrated with everyone dancing around the topic, Ana threw a box on the ground in front of Molly and Cara, and a crying baby added to the mess.

Cara's face went white in an instant. It was the box where she kept old letters from Ronan, stuffed in the back of her closet. Ana then threw the newspaper, *Die Freundin*, and the latest letter from Ronan on top of it. Cara bit her cheek so hard she drew blood.

"You want to embarrass yourself in front of guests now, Cara?" Ana shouted over the screams of the baby.

"We must go, Molly. Cara and her family have some things to sort out," Declan said, grabbing Molly by the hand to take her out of the flat.

"Wait! They're mine! That newspaper is mine! Cara was holding it for me," Molly attempted. The room was silent for a beat as the baby had calmed down.

"While I appreciate the desire to defend Cara, unfortunately, we know this is what she is doing. I believe this disease has been passed down from her brother. We are so sorry you have had to witness this perversion in addition to the difficult day you have had," Ana said.

Cara locked eyes with Molly again before Declan dragged her out, the door closing behind them.

Chapter 7

When Ronan turned eighteen, he moved closer to Trinity University, where he was accepted on a scholarship. Unfortunately, when his Da died a scant year later, Ronan took it upon himself to return and be the head of the O'Shea household. This meant finding work to help support his family. He spent time with Catherine, Molly's mother, asking if he could work with Declan to build railroad lines.

Declan could not return home for Ronan's Da's funeral, but Catherine assured him that when he did come home, Ronan could go with him to the next job to assist. He understood it would mean being away from his family, but at the very least, he could bring money home. He figured he would be guaranteed a job if he could get in Catherine's good graces. In the interim, Catherine suggested he look for work at St. Kevin's. The parish office needed someone to file records or organize the church's event calendar.

Ronan walked into St. Kevin's parish office to find three ladies; he guessed they were in their sixties. He remembered occasionally coming into the office as a child. On his return, he noticed the women seemed frozen in time, maintaining their gray hair, wrinkles, and thick spectacles. At first, when he entered the office, he grew scared that they would scold him like they did when he was a child for taking too many toffee pieces out of the candy jar.

However, they welcomed this bright new presence of a young man returning from university to help his family. They hired him on the spot, and he started the same day, helping them with filing and planning summer fundraisers. Once he was established, they brought him cakes, pasties, and other treats for his family to show their appreciation. The only feedback Ronan ever received was that it was nice having a strong young man around, someone to reach the tallest filing cabinet or move heavy boxes.

So, when Declan returned from a job and asked if he wanted to join him on his next trip, Ronan had to think about it. He returned to the one-room flat his family had rented, resulting in being down to just his income. He addressed this with Cara, who was only sixteen at the time. Ronan was three years older, but they were still close, more like best friends than brother and sister. He sat down at the kitchen table, an old handmade wooden relic from one of the office ladies.

"Declan has asked me to go with him on his next job," he confessed to Cara, "it would be a lot more than I am bringing home now. We may be able to get out of Henrietta Street." He brushed back his red hair.

"I cannot see you performing manual labor," Cara said plainly, avoiding his eyes and peeling the paint off the table.

"I am only slightly insulted by that statement," Ronan teased.

However, instead of a smirk or laugh, Cara's eyes began to well up.

"What is it, now? Buck up. I can handle it," he said.

"It's stupid," she confessed.

44

"You can tell me," he said, and he meant it.

"I don't want you to go away. It's great having you here. Gran doesn't pick on me as much. Maggie loves you, and Ma is about to give birth, so she'll be busy with the baby. I can't talk to anyone my age because I can't relate to them anymore," she confessed and wiped away tears streaming down her face.

"You've been talking to Molly," Ronan observed.

"Sure, Molly. But everyone else I was friends with has stopped talking to me like I am to be pitied now that I am poor and without a father. I need you here."

Ronan thought about this. The money from the rails could afford the family a better life. However, what kind of life would he be living?

"Okay, I'll stay," Ronan said.

"You will?" Finally, Cara looked up into his eyes.

"I promise to stay for as long as you need me," Ronan said.

She got up from the table and hugged him tightly. He didn't mention anything to his mother or Gran.

A week later, one of the office ladies told him Father Patrick needed assistance creating the Easter banner. During Lent, the altar boys would carry candles, a cross, and a large banner on a wooden stake. The cloth was heavy canvas and needed reinforcements.

Ronan went to the rectory to meet Father there. He had not encountered him at St. Kevin's before that day, as Father Patrick was new to the parish. His hair was blonde, and his eyes a bright emerald green. He looked about Ronan's age, and his black button-down shirt clung to his chest and biceps in all the right places. When they shook hands, it was as if electricity pulsed through them. Ronan saw Patrick's pupils dilate during the handshake, and his hand lingered on Ronan's.

As it turned out, Patrick and Ronan had quite a bit in common. Father Patrick did his pastoral studies at Trinity, and they knew some of the same people. After the Easter banner was built, Ronan discovered that Father Patrick needed his assistance on a few other projects. At first, it was only a weekly occurrence that Ronan would be called out to assist with a small manual labor task. Then, Ronan would find excuses to go to the rectory to see if priests needed help for the day.

At first, their affections were seemingly unnoticeable gestures.

Patrick and Ronan were busy installing new wood floors in the rectory kitchen. One of the parishioners made a sizable donation to replace the rotten wood in the rectory. Patrick had asked to show Ronan how to properly hold a hammer, grasping his hand on top of his. Even though Ronan knew very well that learning how to hold the hammer correctly would not be necessary for the task at hand, he allowed Patrick to show him all the same. Then, Patrick invited Ronan to play cards with him after work. Although they were in the rectory common room, the other priests were off eating dinner together in the kitchen. Father Patrick sat close to Ronan, and when Ronan lost, he buried his head in Patrick's chest, pretending to cry. Patrick lifted Ronan's head and met his eyes. Ronan leaned closer to brush Patrick's lips with his own. However, they were interrupted by a roar of laughter in the kitchen, making them both jump. They separated quickly.

The following day, Ronan went to work. He was carrying a bouquet he had stopped to get for the ladies, and as he was placing them in a glass vase, he noticed an envelope with his name on it. One of the ladies said it was a thank you card from Father Patrick for all the extra help he had been providing him with recently.

Glowing, Ronan opened the envelope to discover that although it was a thank you card on the outside, the inside's contents revealed something else. He deflated. Father Patrick would not need additional assistance, and he appreciated Ronan's understanding. He would also appreciate it if Ronan would respect his wish to be with God at this time.

"How kind of him to write me a note," Ronan bluffed. "I shall go down to the rectory to thank him for the card. I will return shortly."

Ronan folded the card and returned it to the envelope before speed-walking to the rectory. He barged inside to find Patrick with his nose deep in his Bible. He looked up at Ronan and shook his head.

"I cannot, Ronan. I am being tempted by sin," he muttered.

Father Patrick rose from the kitchen table, scraping the wooden chair across the recently polished floor. Contrarily, his eyes were sunken and dark, like he hadn't slept. His black ensemble was wrinkled, his hair uncombed.

"You've scuffed the floor, Pat," Ronan said, gesturing to the ground.

"No. No more Pat. No more Patrick. Father Patrick, Father O'Malley, or Father, if you must. I am an ordained priest," he replied.

"An ordained priest who is falling," Ronan whispered.

"Falling from God, perhaps. This is not the same as it was at Trinity. I participated in that sin during my studies but have sworn it off. This is my life, Ronan. I could be in a lot of trouble." He ran his fingers through his greasy blonde hair.

Ronan's heart pounded in his chest, and his mouth went dry.

"If you are fine living this lie, I will leave you."

47

Chapter 8

Gran pulled Cara out of school for the remainder of the semester and sent her to work at St. Kevin's to bring money home for the family. Gran reasoned that if Cara was looking at nude women, then she wasn't learning anything worthwhile to keep her in Catholic school.

Father Patrick kept a close eye on her, never leaving her alone with the nuns, as if she were a predator waiting to pounce on her prey. After all that she had done for St. Kevin's, all the awards she had won, the times she went to confession, the money she had raised when her family barely had enough to feed themselves, this was her penance. They forced Cara to join the choir and sing every mass on Sundays and Saturday evenings.

She would catch glimpses of Molly when she attended, deep bags underneath her eyes, looking like she hadn't slept in weeks.

Then, one morning at mass, she noticed Molly sitting alone in a pew without her father. Cara's heart jumped. Maybe she could get her alone momentarily, at least to say goodbye.

They locked eyes.

After mass, Cara tore off her choir robes and ran to the bell tower. She waited hours outside in the hot summer sun, but

Molly never arrived with the key. Cara watched herself outside her body, kicking a pebble back to St. Kevin's.

As quickly as Irish summer came, it left just as fast, as early September rains dropped temperatures to near freezing. The dreary weather was more appropriate to match the tragedies of the spring and summer.

Every day was the same, and Cara felt like a prisoner in her home. She was not even allowed to go to Hal's, especially after Gran and her Ma had read Ronan's letter and discovered Hal's involvement in the mess. Cara never confirmed that Hal had a ticket to Berlin. She assumed he did. However, it turned out that Hal never received any such thing. He was honest and admitted to hiding the newspaper and being a conduit with Ronan, but he never received a ticket.

With Gran and Ma receiving her pay directly from the church, Cara had no money to plan an escape. In addition, Gran reminded her how daft she could be to assume that traveling to Berlin required one ticket. Berlin was in Germany. Germany required a journey of many ferries, trains, trolleys, and buses. Had she not seen a map before, or perhaps a globe?

Cara felt stupid when Gran presented her with these questions. How could she know what was required of international travel if she had never done it before?

Cara had accepted her new fate, living out her punishment by singing hymns and parish filing. Ronan's charm with the office ladies did not seem to be genetic, and she received no pasties or cakes to bring home despite the two being blood-related. This was fine by her, as she barely ate, living every day trying to survive by passing the time. She only felt joy when her head hit the pillow, and she prayed she would not wake up to face another monotonous day.

Yet, as she walked to St. Kevin's on the fifteenth of September, she felt a warm breeze linger. She had to loosen her buttoned-up cardigan as the sun beat down on her. She arrived at the office to find Father Patrick waiting for her in one of the donated upholstered chairs that almost sank to the ground. She swung open the glass door, perplexed to see him inside sitting.

"What's the craic?" he asked her.

"Did you just learn that word from one of the youths, Father?" she asked with a smirk.

"They do keep me young. I shall rephrase. Where is the craic?"

She stared blankly at him and shrugged.

"Here, Cara. The party is here. We are going to have an end-of-summer lunch outdoors," he said.

"When?" she asked, confused by the sudden desire to hold an outdoor luncheon.

"Today. I was hoping you could go to the market and purchase supplies for a large apple cake that can feed the staff here. We need a morale boost before we enter the dreary fall season. What do you say?"

Cara looked down at him, his green eyes sparkling. "Sure, Father Patrick. I shall go purchase supplies after I get some work done."

"No, Cara. You shall go purchase supplies right now," he said sternly.

She furrowed her brows and rolled her eyes. "Right. Fine. I shall go right now," she said, pushing the glass door open.

Had he talked to her about this yesterday, she could have stopped at the market on her way to the parish office. What would a giant apple cake do for morale anyway?

50

The t-strap shoes she had been wearing that year were starting to wear holes in the bottom of the leather. Cara's hair was unkempt and had taken on its own personality, sticking out in some places and lying flat in others. Most days, she stuck it up in a bun to keep it out of the way. Gone were the days she wrestled it into a neat plait and unfurled it for tangle-free coils. She could not be bothered. Even her current outfit looked drab; once neatly pressed and white, her blouse was now wrinkled and stained a dark yellow underneath the armpits. The only time she bathed was when one of her family members commented on her stench, and even then, the idea of sitting in a tub of water and scrubbing her skin fatigued her.

The walk back on the path she was just on particularly irked her. Her hands were balled into fists, and her shoulders almost touched her ears as she entered the market. Cara did not dare meet anyone's gaze but instead walked ahead with her eyes scanning the ground until she bumped into a rotund belly.

"Pardon me, Miss Pitiful," a familiar voice said.

She looked up, and there he was, a face she had not seen since spring.

"Hal!" she cried out. A smile spread across her lips, something she thought she would never do again. She opened her arms wide and hugged him around his waist, missing his smell, his shop, and his company.

He was carrying a basket full of apples, butter, and flour. She backed away and looked at his basket.

"What a coincidence. I am making apple cake today for a stupid church lunch," Cara said, wiping her eyes.

"I am aware," he said, winking.

She squinted at him and folded her arms across her chest.

"These supplies are all paid in full. Take the basket and go

51

straight to the rectory kitchen. Unpack the supplies and follow the instructions," he said.

"Why couldn't you bring the supplies to the rectory? Why is this so secretive?"

"Let's just say the office ladies are very close with your Gran. Your Gran does not need another reason to be suspicious," he said, looking around him. "Go now, Cara."

Still perplexed by this strange situation, she hugged Hal tightly, grabbed the basket of supplies, and walked quickly back to St. Kevin's.

Chapter 9

The priests in the rectory noticed Father Patrick's scuff mark on the new wood floors rather quickly.

It was the talk of all the priests who lived in the rectory; how could someone be so careless to have scuffed the newly installed wood floors and not attempted to remedy it? Who among them would be the one to repent? Who would be the one to take it out of their menial salary to pay for the repairs? The option to bring in the person who helped install the floors, Ronan, was out of the question, for he had quit working at the parish.

Father Patrick attempted to avoid this talk, excusing himself whenever someone brought it up. He had even tried to get rid of the scuff himself in front of his housemates, sacrificing himself for the good of his living situation, telling the others that all this talk was making a song and dance about it. Jesus would never make such a fuss. Indeed, if Jesus encountered this situation, he would roll up his sleeves and get to work. The opportunity presented itself to make him a martyr.

Unfortunately, this did not go his way, as the varnish lifted, making the appearance much worse. Now, they had to worry about the appearance and the chance of rot setting into the wood floor again. By the end of the week, word had spread to Monsignor, who showed up unannounced to try and make peace within the living quarters.

Monsignor walked into the rectory wearing his black button-up with a Roman collar, black suit coat, black trousers, and a large wooden cross necklace, rumored to have bits of Jesus's cross embedded into it. The buttons on his shirt could barely keep the fabric fastened together around his waist, and the black trousers were tight around his ankles. He had to duck to fit his head underneath the door frame. Behind him walked Ronan, cheeks slightly red from keeping up with Monsignor's gate. The large man pointed to the kitchen floor, where Ronan nodded in understanding.

"This is what the men have been complaining about? This small little chip?" Monsignor said. His voice boomed inside the small kitchen, and those inside the rectory had come to inspect what was happening.

"Monsignor, it is an honor to have you here. We did not know you were coming," Father McKinny said. His eyebrows were bushy and fixed in a permanent expression of disapproval.

"I am surprised to find myself here," Monsignor said, "for a small scuff that this capable young man could fix. Why did no one consult him to fix this when he was the one who installed the floors?"

Father Patrick was in the hallway, attempting to hide and listen to the commotion.

"Where is Father O'Malley?" Monsignor asked.

"I saw him in the hallway," Father McKinny barked.

Patrick pursed his lips and came out of the hallway. "Hello, Monsignor. It is an honor to have you here."

"I am upset to have come from Trinity due to unrest in this parish. It is not what I expect from men of God. Why did I have

54

to find this boy on my own?" he asked, gesturing to Ronan. "I expect you two to work together, primarily to have Ronan show you how to repair the floor so that if this happens again, we know how to fix it. Is it understood?"

Patrick nodded his head silently.

"Good. I am late for dinner, so I must go. I do not wish to hear more about the arguing at St. Kevin's." With that, the Monsignor ducked his head underneath the door frame and went on his way.

"Well, you heard him," Father McKinny barked. "Go to work, you two."

He left with the other priests to return to their quarters, leaving Ronan and Patrick alone in the kitchen.

Chapter 10

Cara dumped the contents of Hal's basket on the rectory's kitchen table. The apples rolled, wobbling to a stop in the uneven grooves. They were sweet apples, bright red and polished with wax to make them shiny. Cara scowled. Sweet apples turned to mush when exposed to the heat. The contrast of tart apples and sweet cake made Cara's apple cake so delicious. Now, with sweet apples and sweet cake, it would be cloying. There weren't even lemons to keep the apples from oxidizing.

With the rush Hal put her in, she expected a note within the basket, perhaps a letter from Ronan she could burn straight after reading. However, there was nothing but apples, flour, sugar, and butter. She sighed and opened the paper flour sack to find a thick envelope covered in soft-milled wheat. She dusted off the flour, and a white cloud bloomed in scattered particles.

"Hello?" she called out to the room.

No one responded to her.

She went out to the living room. "Hello?" she called out again. Then, she went into the hallway where the bedrooms and toilets were.

"Is there anyone here to help me bake an apple cake?"

Silence again. No one was in the rectory with her.

She went back to her kitchen station and took out the envelope. Shaking, she carefully tore open the flap. Peeking inside, she found a stack of thick paper rectangles of various sizes and a note that read, "Your journey begins today. Meet me at Connolly Station."

She placed the envelope and its contents in her cardigan and walked to Connolly Station. When she arrived, she saw Hal with a luggage trunk outside the sizable black locomotive.

"It's a long journey ahead of you, Cara. Ronan will take good care of you. There are benevolent souls to our kind in Berlin," he said.

"Our kind? You are... as well?"

Hal nodded. "Your trunk is packed with clothes for the journey, along with a letter from Molly. Don't forget us plebeians when you become a well-known designer," he said with a smile.

"This is happening so fast." Cara's hands were shaking as she took the trunk from Hal.

"I have the journey mapped out for you in that envelope. Do not lose any of your tickets. Ronan's address is also in there. Send me a telegram if you find yourself in trouble. Understand? You are going to be okay, Cara."

She was crying now, at a loss for words. She hugged Hal tightly, not wanting to let go until she heard the train whistle.

"Go on, Cara. This is your chance to leave this life behind. Go on."

She separated from him and wiped her eyes. Hal took the trunk back from her and handed it to a train conductor, who gave Cara his hand to help her up the stairs. She waved goodbye to Hal and rifled through her envelope to find the first ticket leaving from Connolly Station.

She gave it to the conductor, who showed her where she would be sitting, aptly at a window, where she watched the city disappear into the horizon as the train shuttled toward its next destination.

II

Part Two

Berlin, Germany
1929

Chapter 11

Cara pulled out the paper that had Ronan's address scribbled on it. It read "Ronan O'Shea, Kalckreuthstraße 11, Berlin." She looked up at the address on the front of the building and back down at the address on the paper. The addresses matched, yet she was staring up at a nightclub sign that read, "Eldorado, Hier Ist's Richtig!"

The sign outside had three cartoonish disembodied heads: a woman on top with a fan covering her mouth, the second woman on the bottom right with a square, hard-edged jaw, and a third on the bottom left: a man with a pencil mustache who was winking. They all looked a little cockeyed, and Cara turned her head to meet their gazes.

Her long, curly brown hair caught in the wind, and her handmade tan cloche hat nearly blew away before she grabbed it with a white-gloved hand. The brown freckles on her face were slightly hidden underneath the powder she had put on that morning. She looked up toward the tops of the buildings and saw a steeple in the distance. Again, she checked the paper, "Ronan O'Shea, Kalckreuthstraße 11, Berlin." The building's address matched the note's address, but this looked to be a nightclub, not a residence.

The trunk she carried felt heavier, having been carried blocks

61

from the train station. She heaved it upward by its nearly broken handle and started to walk, a grimace plastered on her face. She quickened her pace as if walking faster would make the weight lighter.

The people of this neighborhood were nothing like she had ever encountered in Dublin. Women had short haircuts and wore the fashion she was chastised for: oversized striped suit coats, trousers with full-size pockets, A-line dresses without petticoats, and exposed bare legs. How could they walk without stockings in their shoes? Did they not get blisters?

Comparatively, Cara wore one of two of the outfits that had been packed for her (the other being a set of pajamas), a particularly outlandish outfit for her arrival: a Kerry green skirt and matching flared waistcoat with brass painted buttons and embroidered roses on the breast pocket. She recognized the stockings shoved inside as hand-me-downs from her neighbor's Spanish cousin, who was twice the size of Cara and darker complexioned.

The bunched, tanned stockings, along with her Kerry green outfit embroidered with sweet roses, drew glances from everyone walking by. The outfit was outrageous enough already in her new cosmopolitan surroundings. However, Cara had altered the skirt and had sewn in a scratchy, coarse, cotton petticoat so she wouldn't have to put it on separately. As she walked, she put her head down and continued, feet shuffling, ears tinged with pink, scratching and pulling at the tight, coarse cotton. She attempted to make herself as small as possible, even though she was fully aware she looked like a character walking out of a forgotten era.

Though the sun was setting early, Cara witnessed the city of Berlin beginning to wake up. Incandescent lights blinked

62

on and illuminated the intricate facades of old buildings with gilded accents rubbing elbows with the modern, sleek elegance of modern buildings. Cable cars hummed in the street, nearly missing the large automobiles parked adjacent to the concrete pavement. Similar to Dublin, these edifices were planted nearly centimeters apart, hugging the street corners, each with its own commanding presence.

Street vendors offered soft pretzels from their carts, a snack before a heavy night of debauchery. The smell of hot yeasted dough and melted butter wafted under Cara's nose. Her stomach rumbled loudly, causing a nearby child to turn his head and stare. She smiled as politely as she could in his direction, but this caused him to start wailing in response. How bizarre she must have looked.

She tried again to pick up her walking pace, but she had not eaten much during her days of travel, and the anticipation of her unknown fate killed her appetite. Tired from lack of sleep and food, she suddenly stopped in the middle of the bustling surroundings, and the Berliners jolted before walking around her, mumbling, "Verzeihung!" She nodded and mumbled back, "Sorry. Pardon me." She moved off to the side so as not to disrupt the flow of pedestrian traffic on the pavement.

She was seemingly wandering nowhere and chewed on her bottom lip as she mulled over her next move, eventually turning around to head back to the address listed on the piece of paper. At the very least, she could ask if anyone knew Ronan. She weaved through the bustling evening crowd once again.

The Eldorado sign snapped on with blinking incandescent lights and neon-tubed accents as if on cue with her arrival. The folding fan of one of the disembodied girls animated back and forth. Cara gaped at the flashes, bathing in the brightness.

Dublin had a nightlife, but this was different.

Out of the corner of her eye, she could see movement. It startled her, and she quickly pressed down on her clothes and dusted off the invisible lint on her handmade outfit. A tall woman walked out of the club's double doors towards her with elegance in every stride, her high heels clicking rhythmically on the uneven cobblestone.

"Guten Abend," the lady said to her.

"Oh, Guten Tag." Her face grew hot. "Englisch bitte?" she stumbled through the words.

"That is quite all right. You will learn German soon enough," the lady replied.

Cara did not speak, and they stared at one another. The woman had a squared, masculine jaw, just like the one in the cartoon above the club, except she wasn't holding a fan but a red Bakelite cigarette holder. She was bundled up in a tan pea coat with fur lining. Underneath, Cara could spot pink tulle spilling outside her coat. Her hair was fashioned in a short, wavy black bob, cropped at her chin. Her nose was long and bumpy, and when the lights flashed over her head, Cara could spot stubble on this woman's face. The lights reflected off her dark, dewy brown skin.

"Honey, you can stare as long as you want. That fanned lady was modeled after me. I'm positively flattered," she said in a thick American accent.

"Oh, that's you?" Cara asked sheepishly. "Beautiful. Do you work here, at this place?"

"Well, I don't do anything for free," she replied, cackling and puffing on her cigarette. A cloud of smoke lazily escaped her mouth, and she inhaled it elegantly through her nose.

Cara started to wring her hands, and her cheeks flushed

bright red. "Is this, um, I'm looking for Ronan O'Shea?"

"You poor thing, Cara, dear. Ronan filled us in. We are ready for you, darling." The woman towered over her, and she moved to embrace Cara, who was shaking.

Gran told Cara that she had money at one point in her life and that they grew up with a black house worker. Outside that tale, Cara had rarely encountered someone with dark skin unless it was the occasional visiting African missionary studying in Dublin. She most certainly had never seen a black man impersonating a woman and had never heard of a man dressing in women's clothes outside of the theater, let alone on the street, where there were people around.

Cara initiated pulling back and curtsied to her. The woman lifted one eyebrow and then picked up Cara's trunk like a handbag.

"I'm Edith. We've been expecting you. Ronan's working on some paperwork, but I'll give you a little tour of where you'll be staying. Follow me," she turned around and waved for Cara to accompany her.

Cara froze; her feet would not move forward. Edith held the door open and looked behind her to see Cara frozen. She rolled her eyes. "Oh, don't be scared. I don't bite. You'll have to get used to seeing more of us here at Eldorado. Unless you'd rather be at St. Hedwig's Cathedral, I heard they have a decent convent."

Cara picked up her feet and shuffled toward the entrance.

"That's it. You can do it."

Cara did not look at her when she spoke. "I'm sorry. I haven't— um... I just— I don't know. You know Ronan, you said? Didn't you?"

Edith blew out a big sigh. "You are a piece of work. Let's

65

set this straight, little girl. You can look into my eyes. No, not behind me. Into my eyes. That's it. Now, really look at me. What do you see, hmm? You see that I am a human being, like you, with thoughts, feelings, dreams, hopes, everything. I may be black, I may be in a skirt, but I'm just like you. I know you've had a long few days; you've probably never seen the likes of me before, and when Ronan finds out we've had this conversation, he will jump down my pretty little throat because I promised him that I would be patient with you. But that's not who I am. Now, I'm going to offer you my hand and I will take you upstairs to where Ronan's office is. I do not have any diseases and I have washed my hands multiple times today. Plus, if you love Ronan, you will have to love me too. He is my husband, after all." Edith held out her hand, and Cara took it without hesitation.

"Husband? You're married to him? Is that legal?" Cara blurted out.

Edith shook her head. "You have so much to learn."

"I'm sorry. I didn't mean to— it was not my intention—" Cara started.

"The path to hell is paved with good intentions, Cara. I accept your apology. But you can stop explaining. I know what you've been through, and soon, you will find that you are one of us. It will take time, and some things will shock you, but the best thing you can do for all of us is to have an open mind," Edith said.

"I can do that," Cara said, reaching out to Edith for another embrace, and Edith hugged her back.

"Now, that's a proper hug. Come on, let's go get Ronan."

They entered through the club's heavy double doors. Round tables were peppered throughout the space, with wooden chairs stacked on top. Workers were taking down the chairs and laying down crisp, white linen tablecloths. There was a stage in the front of the club, with scuffs and bits of tape on the floor. People were on the stage, marking a half-hearted dance routine, with lone feathers fluttering between their legs. They scattered to their taped places on the floor, lifting their arms, twirling, and muttering counts underneath their breaths.

"What is this place?" she asked Edith.

"This is a cabaret club," she replied.

"What is cabaret?"

Cara was led into an office where she found a pale-skinned, flat-capped, red-haired man sitting among paperwork. His small, round glasses barely circled the circumference of his eyes, and he looked studious as he poured over papers with large numbers. He wore an argyle sweater vest over a yellowing button up shirt. The sweater had a few pinholes, nothing that Cara couldn't mend in a moment. True to Edith's confession, Ronan had a gold band on his ring finger that matched Edith's.

She gently knocked on the door. He turned around, surprised to see them both standing there. He could always become so absorbed in his work that he would shut the outside world out.

"A Miss Cara O'Shea for you, wondering what cabaret is!" Edith sang.

"Cara! Oh, it's so good to see you. It's been years. You've got so beautiful," he said.

Cara tackled him with a hug, and she started to cry.

"Oh dear, I know, I know. I would have written to you about where you were coming, but I know Gran would have intercepted it." He pulled back and cupped her shoulders, looking into her big, watery, sad eyes. "Oh, you poor thing," he wrapped her back in his arms again.

67

Her shoulders began to shake as choking sobs erupted from her small frame. "I'm sorry, Ronan. I'm happy to see you; there's just so much that's happened," she cried.

Edith pulled out a chair for Cara to sit on and grabbed a blanket from one of the dark wooden cabinets in the office. She wrapped her in it gingerly and then held her face in her hands before kissing her on the forehead. She also had tears in her eyes. "You are safe here. Have you eaten today?"

Cara shook her head.

"I'm on it," Edith winked at her.

Moments later, Edith returned with a large tray complete with a soft pretzel from the vendor, a sausage roll, and a steaming cup of tea.

The strangeness of a foreign country, unfamiliar people, a different language, and a surprising setting settled heavily on Cara's chest, constricting her breathing. She gasped for oxygen, but the air was thick and stale.

"Drink the tea, Cara," Ronan said.

She did as she was told and grimaced at the taste. "What is that?"

"It's called a hot toddy. What do you think?" he asked.

She took a deep breath, finally able to calm herself, and drained the entirety of her mug.

"That's my sister!" Ronan exclaimed and ruffled her hair. Cara chuckled at this, and the room suddenly became brighter. Edith smiled and opened a window. The cool air allowed her to breathe more evenly.

"That feels wonderful," she sighed.

Edith refilled her mug with tea, hot water, and whiskey.

"Do you want to talk about it?" Ronan asked.

"You don't have to if you don't want to," Edith said sternly

68

in Ronan's direction, shooting daggers at him. "She's been through so much. Leave her be."

"How much do you know?" Cara asked.

"Gran sent a long letter detailing how the pervert's disease was contagious, and I had infected my sister. That was fun to read," he said.

"I was not allowed near the nuns when I worked at the parish this summer," Cara revealed.

"We can talk more about it later if you'd like. For now, let's take you to where you'll be staying," Ronan said, catching the cue from Edith.

They got up and walked out of the small office. The hallway was decorated with floral wallpaper, some bits peeling at the edges and yellowing. They turned the hallway corner into a small room with a plain twin bed and a simple red fleece blanket tucked into the mattress. Cara scanned the modest accommodations until something spectacular caught her eye: a shiny black sewing machine with a large wooden cabinet and chair, the word *Singer* painted in gold, and intricately painted flowing gold decals in the center and the sides.

"This is an American home sewing machine," Cara squealed, "I was hoping they'd make something like this here. Oh my God! Can I touch it?"

"Well, surprise! It's yours! You can do whatever you want with it," Ronan smiled.

"What?" she exclaimed. "Say I am dreaming!"

She ran her fingers over the lettering and saw the manual next to it. She eagerly flipped through the pages.

"I always remember you hunched over on that awful, plaited rug, mending our clothes," Ronan said, "I hope this isn't too much to ask upon your arrival, but we are desperate for a costume designer. We can't pay you much, but you'll have a place to stay, food, and any supplies you need money toward to make costumes for the shows. What do you say?"

Cara couldn't seem to close her mouth. She embraced Ronan, and they both jumped up and down like kids again. "This is my dream, Ronan. You know it is!" Cara said. She pulled away from Ronan's embrace and looked down at the floor. "You have no idea what you saved me from."

Ronan tilted Cara's chin upward and looked into her eyes. "Let me guess. A life of false piety, marrying whoever asks first, having babies when you are one, never being able to see outside your home, all your days running together, stinking of chamber pots and baby puke? I think I know a thing or two. You escaped so you can be you."

They hugged each other again, tears running down Cara's face. When they let go, Cara snatched Ronan's hat. "Let's put this machine to the test," she said, wiping her eyes.

"Thank you. I've been trying to get him to throw that thing in the trash. Work your magic," Edith said, leaning against the doorway, observing them, hand over her heart.

"We'll leave you to get unpacked," Ronan said.

"We'll also leave you with the whiskey," Edith said and handed over a flask to Cara. "If that isn't gone by the time I come back, we're sinking back a few over dinner," she teased.

"Yes, ma'am. I promise it will be gone," Cara said.

Cara did not unpack but instead pored over the Singer manual on top of her fleece blanket. She read through the first twenty pages before falling asleep fully clothed. When she woke up, a different blanket was placed on her, and she searched the room for a clock. She heard loud music and applause coming from downstairs. She decided to venture down to the club and checked her hair in the mirror before doing so. She realized that she was still in her Kerry green ensemble. Disgusted, she ripped the skirt off and threw it in the bin. She wanted to do the same with the jacket, but decided to place it on her bed. It was cold in Berlin, and this was all she had for now.

Someone then knocked on her bedroom door. Cara walked over and cracked the door open. It was Edith.

"Hi, sorry, I'm trying to find something to wear that doesn't look like I stepped out of the 1800's," Cara joked.

"Check your wardrobe," Edith said. "Can I come in?"

"I'm a woman pervert, and I'm half naked. Just so you are warned," Cara said sardonically.

"Oh, honey, if I ever meet that grandmother of yours, we are going to have a talk."

Cara opened the door for her, and Edith walked over to the petite wardrobe. She opened it and revealed two knee-length dresses with a drop waistline. One dress was black silk with a white "V" that went from the shoulders to the point at the belly button. It also had capped sleeves. The other was an intricately beaded silver tank dress.

"These are stunning," she said, "I've only ever seen these in magazines."

"I figured you may need something a little more normal. It's nothing fancy tonight; I'd go with the black one," Edith said.

＊ ＊ ＊

Cara sat in the audience that night and observed her first cabaret performance. There were women dressed as men, men dressed as women, and Edith herself performed a number

71

where she had tassels on her nipples and swung them around in circles. She even had one circling clockwise and the other counterclockwise simultaneously. Cara's jaw nearly reached the floor observing this, but she could see she also had her work cut out for her. Some of the costumes she observed from the audience had gaping holes and looked well-worn from many performances.

As the last performance wrapped up, she looked at the time. Three in the morning. She climbed the stairs into her new bedroom, excited to start her new life.

Chapter 12

Cara spent the first week at Eldorado with Ronan, observing the show backstage. The performers needed assistance changing, fixing costumes at the last minute, and adding their final touches to go on and perform. Whenever a performer danced outside of the audience view, they rushed toward Cara, and she dressed them according to the show notes. The quick-change garments lined up neatly on hangers. As she became intimate with the performers and the costumes up close, the reality and ingenuity of regular household items appeared to be the only thing holding these ensembles together. She saw it all: paper clips, paste, hair pins, all quick fixes so the performers could move on with the show. The performers initially made their own performance attire. However, as the club became more popular, there was little time left to sit down and sew something.

After the weekend performances, she spent Sunday sketching ideas for making the outfits more functional for the stage and dazzling for the audience, considering the interviews she facilitated with every performer and their understudy. The Germans were blunt. Aesthetically, anything would be better than what they were currently working with, even if some of them did not wear much at all. She needed to address the costumes' functionality first.

Was costume the right word? Cara needed clarification. When the performers left the stage, they also lived this lifestyle. For example, some would casually mention wanting a customized wardrobe they could wear after hours. Although suits were becoming more popular in women's fashion, they were rarely tailored for women. Additionally, some of the women wound painter's tape around their chests to flatten their breasts and would carry on a few days with this before painfully peeling it off.

Cara's first change was to create the cast show pieces and versatile pieces they could wear every day. This new life absorbed her completely. After falling asleep in the early mornings' small hours, she woke up in the late afternoon with the Singer manual pages stuck to her cheek.

Cara avoided spending too much time alone, as inevitably, when she paused, the grief swept over her. Molly's note still lay in her otherwise empty trunk, neatly folded and unread. Though she wanted to write Maggie, tears would threaten to spill out of her eyes before even picking up a pen. It was better this way. She made good friends with the bartenders. All tension left her body when the whiskey wet her lips. She transformed from the poor, grieving Irish girl into a lilted, flirtatious lush.

After the first week of observation and learning how to impossibly thread the needle of her machine, Cara got to work. Although the Singer sewed quickly, it only took some of the work out of sewing. For one thing, it only sewed in a straight line. There were finishing techniques and stitches that Cara still had to do by hand, but for the basic joining of material, the needle went through fabric like butter. Setting up the machine proved difficult as well, even having read the manual a half dozen times, and it took Cara a few tries to figure out why she needed a bobbin. The first time she correctly wound it, she darted out of her room to show Edith and Ronan, who both wore a pleased expression but ultimately expressed their uncertainty about why they were being pulled from their work to see the very machine they purchased for her functioning as intended.

It was also quite loud. Between the clicking of the hand crank and the rhythmic forceful tapping of the needle in and out of the fabric, Cara chose her time to sew wisely. Lastly, the machine needed a bit of maintenance. It required weekly disassembly and oiling, which Cara factored into the timing of when pieces would be ready for the shows.

In addition to the chaos of the schedule and job, she was learning a foreign language.

The first German word she learned was *Schwul*, and it took Cara a few times to get the pronunciation correct. There was a sh- a w that felt more like a v, and a weird E-U exercise she had to practice repeatedly to get the correct form of "U" in the word Schwul. German was a complex language, not nearly as flowery as Gaelic or romantic sounding as French. The German language was blunt and without frills.

For example, if Cara needed to sew a bra into a costume for a performing male performer, she needed to sew a booby holder (Büstenhalter). If a performer needed a pair of elegant gloves to take off as part of the cabaret number, she needed to create hand shoes (Handschuhen). However, the word she heard the most around the club and neighborhood was Schwul. She had to ask a few people what it meant, a couple shrugged their shoulders, likely not understanding her initial pronunciation of *shwool.* The performers stared at her, brows furrowed, positively perplexed at what she was talking about. Finally, after a busy day of creating custom patterns for the performers, she went to Ronan.

Ronan was in his office, looking over some bills. His desk was covered with papers neatly stacked in piles with simple glass paperweights on top. A few gray wiry hairs sprouted through his red beard, and his button-up and suspenders looked tired. The wooden desk was shiny and polished, from what she could see from underneath the papers, and there were push pins with tiny scraps of paper around the wall, reminding him of bill dates, order dates, and even what day of the week to record bar inventory. Compared to the rest of Eldorado, Cara thought anyone could take the office and plop it randomly on a map, and they would never find out it belonged to a cabaret club. She knocked on his door gently. He looked up from his stack of papers, his thin wire glasses on the tip of his nose. He peered over them and invited her in. She sat on a wooden chair that screeched against the floor when she pulled it out. She said she had a question about a word everyone was saying around the club, the word *shwool.*

"Almost!" he said, "it's pronounced Schwul." He made all the correct sounds and moved his mouth to make the proper EU sound. He broke down the sounds for her, and they practiced the word together a few times.

"It will take me a few times to pronounce it correctly. Now, what does Schwul mean? I hear it around the club all the time," she said.

"It means Schwul," Ronan said. It's hard to explain. There's not really a good translation for English; there's no equivalent word. But it means this—" He put his hand up and made a

76

circular motion. Cara stared blankly at him.

"It means bills? Your office? Say more about it," she said.

"Oh, Cara. Stop being so thick. It means—" he paused, "it means men dressed as women, men loving men, women in suits, women loving women. Eldorado, this club, the neighborhood, and the culture around here are called Schwul."

She thought about this for a moment and said, "There is no shame here. Everything is out in the open, and people do not hide who they are. I think I've even seen a few audience members pay for some... favors...of the performers. This is dodgy, no offense. I'm so confused, and I guess I'm relieved. I feel understood, especially when I see women dancing with women, but at the same time, I feel like if I participate, there is still a chance I will either go to hell or Gran will come out of the walls and chase me with a belt."

Ronan was quiet for a moment.

"You should go to the Institute for Sexual Science on your day off. They hold tours regularly. I think they have certain times for English, but I'm pretty sure everyone there speaks it anyway because they are making big strides in sex research," Ronan said casually.

"Sex research?" she looked shocked.

"My dear, Hal told me he saw you rolling around with your head between a girl's thighs. I should hardly label you innocent. Yes, sex research. Go find out tomorrow."

"He saw us?" she asked, her face flushing.

"I should hardly label a public park a private space," he retorted.

Cara swallowed hard. "I loved her," she said.

Ronan put his hand on hers. "Who was it?"

"Molly," she whispered.

Ronan blew out a breath and squeezed his eyes shut. "I'm so sorry, Cara. I knew you two were close, but I didn't realize—"

"It only recently developed," she said, wiping away a tear with the palm of her hand. "It's so painful. I'm draining your whiskey supply."

Ronan laughed, "You can have as much whiskey as you like. But remember, our lot tends to have a problem stopping once we start. Be careful with using that to deal with your feelings. It will take time, but I promise it will get easier once you have space from it. You'll meet people who are like you. You may even fall in love again." He lifted her chin with his index finger.

Cara half smiled, "I don't know about that."

"In time. You don't have to rush anything. But please go to the Institute. I think you'll be surprised how normal this all is."

Cara left Ronan's office planning to go to the Institute for Sexual Science the following day.

Returning to her bedroom, she opened her wardrobe and pulled out her trunk. Inside, the letter was still neatly folded, inked with her name in perfect penmanship. She took the first one on top and traced over the loopy handwriting with her finger. She smelled the paper, searching for any lingering scent of Molly. The letter was the only tangible object she had left of her, yet she could not bring herself to look inside. Cara tucked the paper back into the trunk and shut the wardrobe.

Chapter 13

Neither Father Patrick nor Ronan spoke to one another those first moments alone.

Ronan walked over to the scuff on the floor and bent down to look. It wasn't much to fuss about, and Ronan knew he could fix it quickly. He rolled up his sleeves and dug inside his messenger bag to find the wood glue. He gently removed the chip from the floor and started filling in the gap with the glue. When he finished, he stood up and put the tube of glue back in his bag. Unfortunately, he would have to return the next day to sand it down and stain it the same color as the floor. Not that Patrick was or would be any help; the entire time Ronan was filling in the gap, all he did was stand behind him and look on. Ronan did not meet Father Patrick's eyes as he wordlessly approached the door. That was until he felt a hand on his shoulder.

Ronan sighed heavily, still not wanting to engage. He turned around but looked down instead of meeting Patrick's gaze. He knew the moment he looked into Patrick's brilliant green eyes, he would unfurl, and his anger toward this cowardly man would melt away. Perhaps Ronan did not understand the gravity of Patrick's vows, or maybe he did not care. What he did understand was the magnetism between them, the heat that was generated between their bodies when they were in the same room. He knew Patrick felt it, too; otherwise, he would not have engaged Ronan so much.

They stood facing each other, Patrick's hands on Ronan's shoulders and Ronan's arms folded across his chest. Patrick traced Ronan's muscular arms with his hands and made his way to his hips, where he squeezed, making Ronan instantly hard.

What were they doing?

Ronan bit his lip hard, hoping the pain would make his erection go away. It had the opposite effect on Patrick, who took it as a sign to crush his mouth against Ronan's. Before he knew it, Patrick walked backward while kissing him, leading them back to his bedroom. Ronan did not think. Neither of them spoke.

Father Patrick closed the door behind them and pushed Ronan onto his small bed. Breathless, Patrick ripped off his Roman collar and threw it on the floor before straddling Ronan. He unbuttoned Ronan's shirt and took off his trousers, kissing down his naked body before fully taking him into his mouth.

It didn't take long for Ronan to climax. Breathing heavily, Ronan grabbed Patrick back up to his face, and he collapsed next to him. Ronan propped himself up on his elbow and finally looked Patrick in the eyes. They smiled at each other, and Patrick took his thumb and brushed it over Ronan's lower lip.

"I have a confession to make," Father Patrick whispered.

"Forgive me, Father, for I have sinned?" Ronan teased.

Patrick shook his head. "I love you."

Then, there was a knock at the bedroom door. Both of their faces filled with panic.

"Everything alright in there, Father?"

Patrick put his hand over Ronan's mouth. "Fine! Getting in a workout is all. Need to stay trim," he replied.

The doorknob turned.

"No need to come in!" he said.

It was too late. Father McKinny opened the door to find a naked Ronan and Father Patrick lying together.

Chapter 14

The Institute was in Tiergarten, in the same neighborhood as Eldorado. Cara wore her newly crafted tweed trousers with deep pockets, a white flowing blouse, and a tan trench coat with soft interior checkered lining and a tie around the waist. The best feature of her ensemble was that all her belongings were spread among her deep pockets. The outfit was her first project on the Singer, and although there were some crooked stitches here and there, Cara wore her outfit with her chest out, taking long, confident strides on the cobblestone street. It was the end of October, and Cara had been in Berlin for a few weeks. Despite her best intentions to get to the Institute earlier, it took her some time to recuperate from her long journey.

She approached the steps of the Institute and swung the door open to find a man with round spectacles and an equally rotund stomach waiting in a leather armchair. He turned to look up from his book, his thick mustache moving as his mouth did.

"Are you the new designer at Eldorado?" he asked, closing the book he was reading and standing up.

Cara beamed at being called a designer. "I am. I'm Cara," she held out her hand.

He took it delicately and pulled her in to kiss her on both her cheeks. "I am Magnus. It is a pleasure," he said. His English was nearly perfect, with little trace of an accent. "I will be leading your tour today. Shall we begin?"

"Should we wait for any others?"

"This is a special private tour for you. By request of a good friend of mine, your brother," he replied.

She smiled a knowing smile. "Thank you. I appreciate this, I really do."

Although there was no one in the hallway, she was led into another room full of plush cushioned chaises and couches in luxurious jewel tones of purple and green, leather armchairs, colorful rugs, exotic art, and people all around engaging with one another. Some of them were cuddling, and some of them were engaging in heated discourse. Her eyes widened, and her stomach became tight, like when she first met Edith. Magnus gestured to a well-worn leather chair as if picking up on her cue.

"Sit down," he said, "I heard you like whiskey."

Cara nodded and took a seat. Knowing the reaction she received when she first met Edith, she looked down at her hands folded on her lap. She and Edith mostly minded one another around the club, but she still could not get over the shock of her saying Ronan was her husband.

Magnus sat down next to her and handed her a glass of whiskey with ice. She marveled at the inside of the glass. She had ice in her icebox at home, but it was in large blocks to keep food cold. These were small cubes inside her drink. She raised one eyebrow before taking a sip. The whiskey burned the back of her throat, making her cough.

"You should wait until the ice melts in your drink. It will be smoother then," he said.

"I have never seen ice so small before!" she choked.

Magnus let out a hardy laugh, "I do enjoy these small luxuries. Soon, you will, too."

Cara stared into her glass and tried not to look at the people in the room. Magnus noticed.

"Let's have a conversation. I understand you come from a religious background. You have much to learn about how other people live their lives. Are you open-minded?"

Cara remembered the conversation she had with Edith.

"I am. I have so many questions. I feel naïve, perhaps, sheltered from this world," she admitted.

Magnus then told her about his work as a professor, doctor, and researcher. He studied how humans are biologically born with predetermined sexual attractions and that gender is not only female and male. This last bit was highly confusing for Cara. She was a female, but she felt like a girl despite wanting to wear trousers with pockets.

"Think of it this way," Hirschfeld started, "if you could dress in trousers back home, would you?"

"Of course, I would," she said.

"That is outside traditional female sexual expression!" he exclaimed, "just as Henry over there," he gestured to a person with a drawn-on pencil mustache and large hips, "feels that he can be his most joyful self with facial hair."

Henry tipped his hat toward Cara and winked at her. Cara forced a smile and looked back down at her hands. These people all seemed so silly to her.

"Is this not illegal? Or perhaps immoral?" she asked.

"Expression is not immoral; it is biological. It is within our human nature. The reason that religion tells us otherwise is to have control over us. It is easier to placate the masses when everyone plays by the same rules and fits into neat boxes," he said, taking a long drink from his glass.

"So, my relationship with a woman?" she questioned, expecting Magnus to scrutinize her. She looked up, and all she saw was understanding in his eyes.

"I am afraid my relationship with a woman was perhaps the cause of her mother's death," she blurted out, tears threatening to spill out of her eyes. "What if the devil won and God is punishing us?"

"That is not a kind and merciful God," he said plainly, "did you love her?"

Cara nodded her head. She chewed on the inside of her cheek and picked her cuticles.

"The love that I have for her was real. I've never felt like that with anyone else, and I am not sure I could, the least of which with a man. However, I cannot move past the guilt and shame. I wish I could live a normal life and start over, to have never allowed myself to feel this way," she said.

"When the world tells you from the time you are born that your very existence is shameful, you subconsciously or unknowingly start to believe it. As you unpack this shame and guilt and realize that others around you were ignorant of how nature is, you may still feel shame and guilt because you have absorbed this message your entire life," he said, crossing his legs.

Cara took a long sip of her whiskey.

"Nature isn't like this?" Cara asked.

Magnus smiled.

"I hope you like to read," he replied.

Cara left the Institute with a stack of books, and even though the thick tomes weighed her down, she glided back to Eldorado as if on air. If Magnus was correct, then there was much more to unpack than her relationship with Molly. It would mean that the adults she trusted to keep her safe were, in fact, fallible. If Magnus were wrong, though, she would indeed feel God's wrath.

In addition to the reading, she promised to write down any time she felt shameful for a thought or feeling. She joked that doing so would require the paper of all trees in the Black Forest.

Over the next few weeks, Cara focused on her readings, making costumes, and her feelings. She wrote daily about how she felt, the readings, and how they applied to her life. Doing so tapped into her grief, homesickness, and heartbreak, and she even wrote about how guilty she felt over having these feelings. She wrote until she broke the tip of her pen and spilled ink all over the pages. She wrote until her hand was cramped and calluses formed on her fingers. Tears would spill out of her eyes and blur the ink on the page, but it did not phase her. She returned to the Institute weekly and burned her written pages in their fireplace, a cleansing ceremony that Magnus and her community encouraged. On one of her visits, she brought the letter from Molly. Bringing it to this newfound community gave her courage.

"I want to read it," Cara said, "oh, I can't. Someone please read it for me."

"I'll read it," Edith said, her hand on Cara's shoulder. They had grown closer the more Cara learned about gender and sexuality. She held out her palm, and Cara delicately placed the note on it.

My Silly Little Fairy,
I will always love you, even though we are beyond a world apart.
Yours,

86

Molly

Cara held out her hand to take the letter from Edith. There it was, in Molly's handwriting. She folded the piece of paper and tucked it into her shirt pocket, close to her heart.

"I miss her," Cara said.

"You should write to her," Edith encouraged.

She took a seat in Cara's armchair, and Cara put her head on Edith's shoulder. Edith embraced her and Cara let out a soft sob. She wasn't sure if anyone would ever love her like Molly again.

Chapter 15

One day, Cara was busy fixing clothes for the show that night. After designing and creating brand-new costumes for the performers, she had some downtime and finally had time to mend Ronan's hat and make him some new shirts. She promised Ronan she would be quick with the cap, as he was not thrilled to expose the bald spot on the back of his head, so she pinned the new bits of fabric and moved her hands nimbly and quickly. She was interrupted by a knock on her door. It was Ada who ran the stage lights. Cara noticed Ada while working with one of the performers rehearsing on the stage. She was pinning a strap when a bright light shone on her face. Startled, Cara nearly cursed her out until Ada turned the light off and waved at her from the stage deck. She was tall, thin, and had large red lips that Cara was tempted to kiss.

"Sorry about that!" Ada said.

Cara nodded at her and stopped pinning the performer's strap. She was frozen like the day she entered Eldorado. "Can I move now?"

"Sorry. Just a moment. There!" she said and then moved off the stage.

Cara had continued, albeit making careless errors in costuming the rest of the rehearsal. And now, Ada was in her room, asking to come inside. Cara's stomach plunged when she entered.

"Hi, Cara. I was wondering if I could ask you a favor?"

Ada was wearing a pale yellow button-down shirt, suspenders, and trousers that were starting to sag on her. She saw the point of the suspenders. Still, Cara could see a waist underneath all that material.

"Of course. I can help with anything."

"Anything? I will keep that in mind," Ada said.

Was Ada flirting with her? Her cheeks flushed.

"I was wondering if you could bring in my trousers. I got them at the secondhand store, and I love them so much, but they are too big. I need them taken in a little."

Cara snapped into seamstress mode, grabbed her measuring tape, and asked Ada to come closer to her so she could take her measurements.

"Is it okay if I measure you?" Cara asked politely.

"You can do whatever you want to me," Ada replied boldly.

She had never heard a woman hit on her so bluntly before. If her work with Dr. Hirschfeld had taught Cara anything, it was that her desires were natural. She engaged with Ada curiously and playfully.

"That is a tempting offer," she said as she circled the measuring tape around Ada's waist. She marked down the measurement.

"I need to measure the inseam," she said.

Ada stared into her eyes intensely.

"I need you to, um," she blushed. I need you to spread your legs apart so I can get that measurement."

Ada never broke eye contact as she slowly moved one foot,

89

then the other, apart. Cara took the top of the measuring tape and placed it near Ada's crotch, feeling the heat. She traced it down to the bottom of the trouser leg, which was a little longer than it should be.

"I think," she said in almost a whisper, "I think I should hem these as well."

Ada nodded, "I do need these hemmed."

Cara wasn't able to control her smile. "I need to mark it with pins. And then you'll need to take the trousers off and give them to me."

Ada smiled back at her, "Are you trying to get me to take my trousers off, Cara?"

Cara opened her mouth in a fake, flirtatious accusation, "You're the one who wants her trousers to fit. I don't make the rules of sewing. I'm telling you how it works here."

"Well, Miss Cara O'Shea, I think I'd like to get to know you a little better before you start making more striptease demands of me," Ada replied.

Ronan walked into the room at that moment and looked at both she and Ada, who were incredibly close to one another. Cara realized, to her horror, that her fingers were still very much on Ada's crotch inseam. She quickly pulled the tape away, jumbled it up, and threw it back on her desk. Ronan stood in the doorway looking at her, then at Ada.

"Showtime, Cara. Five minutes. We need you backstage. And Ada, lights, let's go. Maybe continue this later."

They both left the room and headed to their stations. Cara grabbed a paper fan backstage and started fanning herself furiously, needing to focus on the upcoming shows. The interaction was so intense and happened so fast. Hers and Molly's relationship was back and forth with confusion and shame. And even when it did get going, it didn't last very long. Where Molly was a slow burn, Ada was an explosion.

The show went on, and Cara was on autopilot. There was a quick fix here and a quick change there, and then the night had finished. Her stomach started to flip again because she sometimes ran into Ada at the bar, grabbing an after-work drink. Cara rushed upstairs to put away her supplies before she could go to the bar, but she found a surprise waiting for her outside her door: Ada.

Cara's breath caught in her throat when she saw her leaning on the wall, smoking a cigarette elegantly in her long trouser suit. Her blonde hair was nicely curled to the side in flapper-girl fashion, and she wore a black beret. Her top buttons were undone, exposing her lace bra. She was a perfect combination of feminine and masculine. Before Cara could say a word, Ada put out her cigarette, gently cupped Cara's face, and kissed her. The kiss was intense and animalistic. Cara let go of all her inhibitions, all the guilt, all the shame. She had burned it all in the fire.

They couldn't tear their clothes off fast enough, and when it came time to get in bed, Cara knew precisely what to do. She kissed down Ada's body, her breasts soft and supple, gently sucking on her pink nipples before trailing down to her wetness. She caressed her gently with her tongue, making note of any sensitive spots. Ada's breath grew rhythmic, and she moaned in anticipation. As shock waves pulsed through her body, Ada uttered words in German that Cara had never heard before. Afterward, Cara rested her head on Ada's pelvis while Ada played with her curls, wrapping them delicately around her dainty fingers. They sat in silence, breathing in sync and anticipating the other's next move.

Ada propped up on one elbow, and Cara shifted so she was under her, Ada gazing into her eyes. Finally, she spoke and promised to kiss every freckle on Cara's body, that she was very determined to find them all. They kissed again, deeply and slowly. Ada didn't seem to mind kissing her after they had made love. She traced circles around Cara's nipple with her finger, and Cara shivered at her touch. Goosebumps formed on her skin, and her hair stood up.

"It's your turn," Ada cooed in between kisses, "I can't wait to find out what makes you feel good," she said, her voice deep and sensual.

Cara blew out a breath. The sexual intensity of their connection was almost more than she could handle. Ada was confident and unafraid to say what she wanted, but it could be an act. Cara had to be sure.

"You know..." Cara began, "If you don't want to, you don't have to. I'm weird, I like, well, you know. I like giving. But I know it can be gross."

"Gross?" Ada furrowed her brows, "what do you mean?"

"Well, it's not to everyone's taste, I guess," Cara said.

"Let me guess. The last person you were with did not return," she said in a thick German accent.

"How did you know?" Cara asked, her cheeks flushed with embarrassment. Ada rolled her eyes and shook her head.

"That girl was not one of us. She was too ashamed and tried to pass her shame onto you," Ada said.

She then pulled the covers away from her body, revealing herself fully nude to Cara.

"I am not ashamed," she said, "and what excites you excites me."

She then put her hand down into Cara's wetness, pulled it

92

out, licked her fingers, and moaned.

"You taste exceptional. I would like more, please," Ada said.

Cara's eyes grew dark, and she spread her legs wide. Ada smiled and stroked Cara's wetness with her hand before diving in with her mouth. Before, Cara could only imagine what it felt like for someone to be with her so fully. She let her head tip back and enjoyed Ada's warmth inside of her.

They stayed up the entire night, making love to each other and eventually falling asleep in each other's arms. The next day was Sunday, a day that the club was closed, and they spent half the day naked, giggling, talking as if they had been lovers for years. Cara couldn't get close enough to Ada. She wanted to be inside of her skin; she wanted to be utterly consumed by this beautiful woman. Eventually, as the afternoon light faded into dusk, Ada told Cara she had to go home to feed her cat. He had been neglected for too long and, according to her, would start to protest by leaving her "presents" around the house if she was away for longer than a day. Other than that, she confessed, he was a sweet cat.

"Maybe I could meet him one day?" Cara asked slyly.

"I think he'd love you," she said and winked. Ada started getting dressed in the clothes she wore the night before, attempting to find all the pieces that had been torn off in a horny fury.

"I'll need you to take those trousers off again at some point so I can fix them," Cara said.

"You know I just used that as a reason to come talk to you," Ada said.

"No, I know that now. But they do need to be taken in. I'll fix them for you."

"I promise to return with the trousers. You are adorable. I'll

93

see you tomorrow, I hope," Ada said.

"You know where I live," Cara winked at her.

Cara waited anxiously for Tuesday to arrive when Ada would come in and start blocking for the show. Would Ada come in early to say hi to her? Cara tried to stay busy. She had a few costumes to mend, but they would only take a few minutes, and her stomach tied in knots with anticipation. She was wringing her hands and staring into space most of the afternoon.

"This is ridiculous," she said out loud. She grabbed her thread and started to thread the sewing machine. She was going to get to work and take her mind off things. She placed a bit of cotton fabric and started the machine going slowly, but then her mind drifted again; the fabric started to be sewn nearly off the machine, and her guiding hand–

"Goddammit!" she shouted. The needle of the machine had gone clear through her finger. Blood started to bloom on the white cotton fabric. Ronan ran into the room and saw her finger punctured clear through with a needle.

"Cara! Are you okay?" Ronan asked.

Cara was clutching her hand as blood poured out of the cracks of her fingers.

"I'll be fine," she said weakly, "It's a little pain, nothing to worry about," attempting to hold back tears.

Then, Ada walked into her room, stunned at the sight of blood gushing out of Cara's punctured finger. She was hours early for her shift, and from what Cara could make out of her clouded vision, she was holding a bouquet of gorgeous sunflowers.

"Oh God. This is so embarrassing," Cara said, still clutching her hand.

"We need a medical kit," Ada said, "Ronan, I think we have

one in the lighting department; I'll grab it and be back."

Ronan walked over to Cara and knelt.

"You need to show me how bad it is," he said.

"I do this all the time. You are making too much of it. It hurts more than it usually does probably because it was done with a machine and—" Cara got cut off because he grabbed her hand and turned it over.

To all his horror, the needle was still in her skin. It had sewn itself through her finger, and the needle had gone through her pointer fingernail and the tip. Blood dripped all over the machine and the costumes, and Cara began to drift in and out, not responding to some of the questions he was asking her. Finally, she stopped responding altogether.

When she woke up again, her finger was bandaged, and she looked up at the ceiling. She thought her hair was being played with.

"My love. How are you feeling?" Ada asked sweetly.

"I'm not dead?" Cara asked.

Ada laughed a deep belly laugh.

"My dear, no one dies from a small sewing needle. Perhaps if it was through the eye socket, but no, I think you'll live to see another day," she said.

Cara lifted her bandaged hand. Her pointer finger had been carefully wrapped with gauze and tape.

"Leave that on for a little bit. Ronan gave you the rest of the night off. Quite a bit of dramatics are happening. Are you sure you don't want to be on the stage?" she asked.

"Who did this?" she asked, pointing to her bandaged finger.

"I did. I trained as a nurse but left the profession. They do not understand women dating their female colleagues. Anyway, I always keep a small medical kit with me. It's quite useful," Ada said matter-of-factly, "but you must have hurt yourself because you were distracted. What were you thinking of before your accident?"

Cara smirked, "you want me to show you?"

"Oh! You must be feeling better, then," Ada said, leaning down so she was in front of Cara's face, whispering, "I couldn't stop thinking about you."

They kissed deeply, leaving Cara wanting more.

"You are so beautiful," Ada kissed her, "But I must go, love. He did not give me the night off." She went downstairs to start the show.

Cara and Ada were inseparable after the incident of Cara's sewn finger. It started to scab over, and she could still sew despite the shakiness she experienced the first time back on the sewing machine. Mostly, when she and Ada were together, they would make love and talk, make love and talk, and repeat this process until one of them had to leave the other.

Cara never met Ada's cat, as she was never invited to Ada's. It was easier this way.

Ada worked at Eldorado and she could come directly to Cara's room when the shows were finished for the night. Ada also never talked to her in front of any Eldorado workers. She expressed wanting to maintain their professionalism. However, she declined when Cara attempted to invite her out during the day, outside of Eldorado, or to the Institute so Ada could meet Magnus or spend more time with Edith. She would say she was busy and find a way to change the subject. Cara assumed it was because they both worked nights, and Ada didn't want to do anything during the day. Perhaps Ada's sleep schedule differed from Cara's. It disappointed Cara that Ada could never commit to anything outside of Eldorado, but despite this, they continued seeing each other.

Chapter 16

Dr. Hirschfeld began a program that winter where he handed out passes to the community, saying men who felt like women and women who felt like men could dress how they wanted outside the clubs and the walls of the Institute. This way, they could be in public and express themselves freely, and if the police stopped them, they would hand out a card stating they were under the care of a doctor. Edith, who had become one of Cara's closest friends, was thrilled with this program, and she was immediately given a pass. This brilliant opportunity afforded the community the ability to express themselves in public. It also opened a new business opportunity for Cara, something that Magnus was keen on her starting.

If the community had medical passes to dress as the gender they felt they were, they would need the clothes to suit them. She found herself at the Institute a few times a week, taking measurements to design garments. She also created one-size-fits-most dresses, tops, trousers, and coats so that if people did not want to wait or could not afford her services, they still had options. Additionally, Dr. Hirschfeld studied medical operations on women transitioning to men and men transitioning into women. Throughout the stages before the surgery, he wanted his patients to have the affirming experience of wearing clothing that brought them joy.

Cara became the entrusted fashion designer for the Tiergarten community. Her heart swelled when her friends scheduled a fitting for a new wardrobe. Soon, on her regular walks to the Institute, she would see her designs worn by her community. No job was too difficult or request too strange for her to fulfill. She started as a silly girl who mended clothes from Dublin and was quickly making her way to being the most prominent fashion designer of the Berlin Schwul.

Still, her favorite work was being behind the stage during a cabaret performance at Eldorado. Nothing compared to the rush of performers piling backstage and getting them ready to perform a number a few minutes later. She didn't even mind the wardrobe malfunctions that happened, causing her to think quickly on her feet and problem-solve for the best solution on stage.

For example, one night, she was stuffing Edith's bra as fast as she could without it piling up over the top. Ronan hung around and watched her, and Cara, annoyed, asked him what he was doing and if he was going to stand there, that he could either stuff or help her sew a piece of stitching that came undone. He had no sewing skills, so he chose to help stuff, Edith, and Edith, in return, giggled and puffed out her chest as Ronan put in pseudo chicken cutlets and tissues. If folks backstage had time to look, they had time to work, and Cara had no shame in giving her older brother orders.

"Cara, I need to talk to you about Ada," Ronan said, awkwardly handling a sticky, rubbery, jiggly fake boob.

"Are you worried about our relationship affecting work? I can keep it professional," Cara replied, starting to sew the split seam.

"It's not about professionalism," Ronan replied, "you're so young and Ada is older. She has a bit of a reputation, and I wanted to—"

"We need to speed this up, as my cue is about ten seconds away," Edith spewed, "Cara, stay away from Ada, she's a bit of a whore, and we don't want you getting diseased the first couple of months you're here. Ouch!"

Cara's hands were damp with sweat, and a pin had slipped through her fingers and accidentally pricked Edith's skin.

"Stop moving, Edith, I'm almost done. There!" she cut the thread, took the pin out, and turned Edith around by her shoulders before giving her a gentle, playful push.

"Break a leg!" Cara waved at her.

Edith turned around, "We're not done with this topic!"

One more yank of her dress up to cover the cutlets, and she was out, shining and singing. Cara had done this so many Saturdays that she could sing the routines by heart. The last performer returned from her number and ripped off her costume, breathing heavily and sweating.

"Water, powder, my next number is the suit number, Cara. I'm so hot it's going to slide off me," she complained.

"Ronan, go get water and powder from the green room, please."

Ronan stared blankly at Cara.

"Water is by the makeup counter, and the powder is on the vanity next to the collection of Jeanette's lipsticks. Let's go; we have two minutes," she said with authority. For being eighteen, she managed backstage well.

Cara prepared the suit and unzipped the back quickly. She oiled the zippers daily so they wouldn't trouble her. They came down smoothly without any snags. She also unzipped the back of the trousers so they were easier to stand in and had Jeanette sit down on a chipped blocking box so that Cara could change out her heels for a pair of black and white wing tips. She grabbed the top hat from the clothing rack beside her and Ronan returned with water and powder. Jeanette chugged the water as Cara powdered her face, not worrying about the mess she was making. She demanded Jeanette lift her arms and put powder on her armpits, and asked if she was ready.

Jeanette took a deep breath and nodded, "Yes, let's put it on."

Cara put the suit front on first and designed the costume to be all in one piece and easy to take on and off. The front had jacket lapels and a button-up shirt cut and sewn into the suit. The back was a zipper that was hidden underneath a piece of the suit fabric. When Jeanette turned around, no one would have any idea that there was a zipper in the back, and that was Cara's intention behind the design. It had taken her a couple weeks to sketch and measure exactly how the garment would work, and she also had a few failures along the way. She had tried to attach the piece of fabric with reusable tape, which was not, in fact, reusable at all. It would get caught in Jeanette's hair, and she also had a wardrobe malfunction in the middle of one of the performances. So, Cara added a zipper, and it worked flawlessly each time. Her next design challenge was to build a garment that could be ripped off without being destroyed. She was still in her sketching stage, but Edith wanted to go more risqué with her performances. The club got busier whenever she showed more skin, so Cara was hard at work figuring out how to make this happen.

She couldn't imagine that it was only a few months ago that Gran had chastised her for designing a suit. Now, she

101

was getting paid to make these innovative garments for the performers and getting the club more money.

Ronan shifted from side to side, and Cara started zipping up Jeanette and getting her back on stage for her final solo. As Jeanette waited in the wings, all dressed and ready to go, Ronan frowned deeply and rubbed the back of his neck, ruffling the red curly overgrowth connecting his head hair to his back hair. Cara slowly turned her head toward Ronan and sighed, audibly annoyed by his presence.

"Ro, I love you. But what do you want from me?" Cara pleaded, "I'm very busy back here, and you're lecturing me."

"Cara, I know you. I know that look in your eyes when you're with Ada. I also know the effect Ada has on girls around here. She's a great worker, but she uses this job to get more girls. Another notch in her bedpost, you know? And you are sensitive and bright and caring, and I don't want you to get your heart broken. She's bad news. She's twice your age!" he cried.

Edith came off the stage, breathing heavily, and looked between Ronan and Cara.

"You're still in this conversation?" she asked. "Ro, you and I have now both tried to talk with Cara. I suppose she's not going to listen to us. Anyway, she's eighteen and naive. Come on, now. Get out of here, leave her alone."

"I'm not naive!" Cara said.

Edith picked up a strand of long, curly brown hair off Cara's head.

"Keep telling yourself that," Edith said, releasing her curl, which sprung back and coiled just as it had before Edith pulled it. She walked off toward the green room.

* * *

Nothing made Cara gloat more than when Ada asked her to Damenklub Violetta's Moonlight Steamship Party. This party, Ada said, was exclusively run by a lesbian who fronted the homosexual rights movement, where there would be drinking on a boat, cabaret, dancing, and a perfect opportunity to take a photo during the sunrise at six in the morning. Ada said it was a wild time and quite romantic. Cara asked how Ada had heard of this, and she told her *Die Freundin*, of course, and Berlin's Lesbisch Frauen.

Cara's relationship with *Die Freundin* was limited, but she was excited all the same. Given how poor Cara's German was, she didn't think she'd ever be able to read an entire issue properly. However, she did enjoy looking at the nude women, so she asked Ada to bring her copies so she could browse them in her free time.

They boarded the ship that evening and departed from Spittlemarkt. Eventually, the boat would arrive in Mugelsee. They would be dropped off at the Ingleshotel for orchestra, dancing, and more. Women were gathered everywhere, boyish-looking women to hyper feminine looking women, some scouting out who was also standing alone, and a few couples snuggling tightly next to one another. Most everyone wore long coats, as winter had not yet broken its nasty cold spell enough for a warm spring. Cara cuddled up to Ada for warmth, but Ada turned away and suggested they talk to other people on the boat. Cara agreed but mostly tagged along with Ada and watched her full, charismatic self come alive. At first, Cara admired watching Ada work the room. The boat started serving Gluhwein, warm spiced red wine, and the hot liquid warmed them up quickly. However, the more Ada drank, the louder she talked. She also started touching people more, and was she…flirting? There was one woman she could not separate herself from; she was in a pinstripe suit and had a haircut like a man's.

"This party is like a dream," the woman in the suit said to Ada.

Cara rolled her eyes.

"Would you like to dance?" she asked Ada. The woman took Ada's hand and kissed it tenderly.

"Would you mind, darling?" Ada asked Cara.

They hadn't talked about being together, just with each other, but Cara did not think she had to. She regretted being trapped in this awkward situation.

"Are you together?" the woman asked, gesturing toward Cara and Ada.

"We work together. Have you heard of Eldorado?" Ada asked, avoiding her question.

Asking if a Berlin Schwul had heard of Eldorado was like asking if a Parisian had heard of the Eiffel Tower.

"My favorite club. How lucky you two work there!"

Cara pursed her lips and excused herself to get more Gluhwein. How quickly Ada turned her affection away from her when they were in public. Her cheeks burned hot with anger, not only toward the woman in the pinstripe suit but also toward Ada, who was all too eager for a new conquest. Cara slipped away to avoid the show between Ada and the stranger. She asked for a second helping of Gluhwein and took it to peer over the ship's railing so she could stare out at the water. The moon's reflection refracted over the waves.

"Your hair," a stranger said, "is gorgeous. I've never seen such curls."

Cara turned to the stranger and wiped tears away. "Thank you. It's quite a bit of maintenance," she replied. "You speak English? How did you know I spoke English?"

"My father was an Englishman. And you don't look German," she said curtly. "Anyway, are you okay? Would you like me to leave you alone?"

"I'm fine. The person who asked me on this boat is flirting with someone else. Right over there," she pointed to Ada and the pinstripe woman, now slow dancing cheek to cheek. "We've been on the boat a whole thirty minutes, and they are getting along just swimmingly. I guess we didn't talk about what we could and couldn't do with us, but I expected different from her. Whenever I think about how far I've come from being sheltered, my sense of tradition and morals slaps me in the face. I'm sorry you don't want to hear all this. I don't know why I'm revealing my soul to you." Cara stared out onto the water.

"I understand. I am the same way with the people I date. However, underneath all this is anything but traditional," the woman replied.

"How do you mean?" Cara looked at the woman. The woman had a pointed chin, clean-shaven, a smaller nose, and shapely eyebrows. Her rouge was the perfect shade of red, a color that Cara had been trying to find for ages for her own skin tone.

"Come on, darling. Look at me. I'm masquerading," the woman said.

"You are doing a damn good job of it. Where did you find that rouge? I've been trying to match my color for ages. It's so beautiful," Cara said.

It was like Cara had found a long-lost friend. The kind of soul connection that happens instantly and intensely. She discovered her name was Marie, but if she needed to, she went by Michael. Marie said she hated Michael and hated who she sometimes had to be when the world was watching. She said she had been coming to the Steamship Party for a few months, and she upped her dressing game every time she did. Cara told Marie that she was a fashion designer and about her intention to work with the founder of the Institute to make custom-fitted dresses and suits for the community. She convinced Marie to get a free wardrobe fitting. Marie grabbed them some whiskey and Cara started to slur and stumble over her words.

The steamboat arrived at the Ingleshotel. It was a large white building with blue shutters and bright, warm, incandescent lights shining through the windows. They could hear the music coming out of the hotel, and Cara was giddy with drink and from making a new friend. Cara and Marie walked hand in hand, disembarked, and walked off the boat up the boardwalk to where the orchestra played Das Lila Lied, or The Lavender Song. Marie started belting out the words in German as loud as she could, and Cara felt shivers run up and down her spine. The song was spellbinding, though Cara couldn't quite make out the lyrics. After the song ended, she asked Marie to translate for her, and they settled in their seats for the orchestra. Marie told her it was a song about homosexual liberation.

"We only love lavender night, which is sultry because we are different from the others."

Marie sighed and looked in the distance as if contemplating the true meaning of these lyrics. Cara's eyes grew wide, and she stayed very still as the crowd joined in singing this song together: a community allegiance. She looked around the room and saw the group's women getting beer steins.

"I want to keep feeling like this," Cara said, "I want beer!"

106

"Why do I have a feeling that you've never had beer before?"

"Because I've never had beer before. My Gran said beer was the devil's spit," Cara said dramatically.

"Then we should get you some of the devil's spit from the devil himself. Bartender!"

Cara continued to drink, and she felt invincible. Everything was so funny, and she felt a strong attraction to Marie. Toward the end of the night, around three in the morning, Cara looked at Marie and pouted her lips.

"What's that about?" Marie gasped.

"I want you to kiss me, please," Cara said.

"Honey, you are gorgeous. I think I failed to mention that I could be your father. I'm around his age, likely," Marie said.

She took a sip of her beer and scratched her chin.

"My father is dead. You are Marie. And Marie is lovely and kind. And I would like a kiss now, thank you," Cara said.

"Darling," Marie lifted Cara's face so she could look into her eyes, "I don't swing that way, but I love you. We should be good friends," Marie said.

Cara pouted but resigned, "Okay, fine." She chugged the rest of her beer.

"Careful, sweetheart. You will be feeling that tomorrow. Make sure you drink some water," Marie said.

"How do you mean?" Cara asked.

"Oh, I bet you've never been drunk before," Marie commented.

"I've been drunk plenty of times. However, when people talk of feeling poorly the next day, I cannot relate to them. I do not feel poorly the next day," she retorted.

"Oh, to be young again. How old are you anyway?"

"I'll be nineteen next month," Cara said, puffing out her chest.

Just then, Ada stumbled over to their table and wrapped her arms around Cara. "Did you enjoy the tombola? Wasn't this night just fabulous?"

Cara let out a gasp as Ada's arms tightened around her neck.

"How old are you?" Marie asked, directing the question toward Ada.

"What a rude question to ask a woman you don't know. But you wouldn't know anything about being a real woman, would you?" Ada spat.

"Marie is my friend, and she's more of a woman than you could ever hope to be. She didn't abandon me to snog some Männin. Talk about not a real woman," Cara replied.

Männin was a word that Marie taught her. It meant a woman who looks like a man.

Ada sat down and looked at Cara. Cara shook her head.

"You're drunk!" Ada shouted.

"So are you!" Cara retorted.

"You let an eighteen-year-old get this drunk? You are trying to take advantage of her," Ada said to Marie.

Both Marie and Cara cackled. What started as a small roll of giggles turned into an all-out, nonstop belly laugh. They clutched their stomachs as tears ran down their cheeks. Ada was confused and kept asking what was happening. Cara wiped the tears from her eyes.

"I was rejected by Marie who told me she's not a Lesbisch," Cara replied.

"Ada, I think that's your name. Ada, dear, it seems that you are the one who has taken advantage of this beautiful young lady and then left her alone on a boat without any company. So, I decided to step in, and we've become fast friends. Why don't you find your lover boy and leave us alone? We were

108

having such a great time until you decided to grace us with your presence," Marie said.

Ada clenched her hands into fists. Cara was starting to figure out the hierarchy within this community. She would have thought that birds of a feather flock together. It turns out that although they do flock together, they also create a pecking order. Ada stormed off and avoided Cara the rest of the evening. After they had calmed down from the disagreement, Cara grew curious about the injustice within their community.

"Why is it that not all Schwul are created equal?" Cara asked, slurring her words.

"Well, isn't that a philosophical and moral dilemma, Miss Cara? I guess for the same reason that some people think Jews like me are of a lower class or people with different color skin. Wherever there are people in a society, there will inevitably be someone who tries to put everyone in a box, and unfortunately, those boxes have different values and rankings. We follow along, and even within our own boxes, we create our own worth and rankings. It's all twisted. I don't think humankind has ever just existed as a community helping one another out. We've always fought or found a way to order ourselves, some with more worth than others."

They sat in silence at that moment, and Cara rested her head on her arms. Marie rubbed her back like a parent would comfort a child who had learned the true weight of the world. The room started to spin for Cara, and she closed her eyes tightly to stop it. The rest of the night went dark.

Chapter 17

When Cara awoke the next morning, she wasn't in her bedroom. The ceiling had gilded gold tin tiles, and the room was flooded with glaring sunlight. Next to the strange bed she was sleeping on, there was a small wooden nightstand, complete with a tall glass of water and two aspirin. The room spun around, and the pain in her head surged against her temples. She sat up and took in her surroundings.

She was underneath a thin felt blanket littered with moth-eaten holes. Her feet moved around, and she could feel crumbs in the bed. The room had parquet flooring, and there wasn't much else besides a bed and a nightstand. She looked behind her and saw a galley kitchen and a modest card table with a vase of flowers on it. She heard snoring, looked down at the floor, and saw Marie sleeping there, with a shadow of stubble and her wig clutched between her hands. Her dark brown hair was only on the sides, and her bald crown was in the middle. A thin coverlet sheet gently hugged her thin frame, and Cara could see a few ribs popping out. Behind the guise of moonlight and drink, she had failed to notice how sickly Marie was, as if she hadn't eaten in weeks, like a walking skeleton.

The world was a strange place. How could someone so thin

110

and frail afford to go on a cruise to a hotel and enjoy a tombola? She supposed it was what Marie prioritized. Although Cara was not wealthy, she was taking on side jobs for the Institute to create clothing. They were paying her extra, and not having to pay for room and board while staying with Ronan was also helpful. She could afford certain luxuries like a night out at a local restaurant or buying herself flowers or materials for both costumes and garments. She didn't bother asking Ronan for money toward supplies anymore. He was already contributing so much. Marie started to stir underneath the thin bed sheet. She stretched wide and opened her eyes.

"Morning, love cake," she said. "Oh, my wig!" she exclaimed, putting it back on her head. " That's better. How are you feeling, darling?"

"I'm feeling dizzy and like I need food. Can I treat you to some breakfast? I know a great breakfast place in Ku'damm," she said.

"Oh, that's quite a ways away and probably a bit out of your budget, dear," she replied.

"It's not out of my budget, and you took care of me last night. It's the least I can do. We can get some fresh air and maybe sweat out some of this poison. I reek of stale beer," she said.

Cara eventually convinced Marie to go to Ku'damm for breakfast. Marie fixed her wig and shaved, and Cara wore the same clothes she wore the night before. On their way to Ku'damm, Marie was stopped by the police, who asked for her papers. She smiled and took them from her bag as they checked that she was legally allowed to be a woman. Although it was revolutionary for Marie to live freely, Cara hoped that one day she could see Marie walk freely without papers, without worrying about the legality of her identity. Why was her

111

existence a police concern?

When they sat down to breakfast, Marie shifted nervously. Cara looked at her and noticed she was trying to sit on her hands.

"Marie, get whatever you want. Seriously. If you want lunch and dinner to take home, please, by all means," she said. Cara knew what it meant to go hungry.

Marie blew out a breath. "It's just I can't decide between the schnitzel and the eggs. But then there's the kugel, and I love kugel," she said.

"Get it all, I don't care. The sky is the limit. Order the whole menu," Cara said.

Marie ordered a large breakfast, and Cara had never seen someone eat so ravenously in her life. She ordered rolls, meats, cheeses, and eggs, all with a side of jam and butter. Cara ordered an egg and a roll and watched Marie devour all the food. When she was full, Marie started stuffing rolls in her purse.

"Marie," Cara touched her hand gently, "you don't—"

"I won't be a charity case. I can see how you're looking at me," Marie retorted.

"I'm not going to hand you any money freely, but if you need a hot meal, I'm happy to provide one," Cara said.

Marie took a breath, held it in, and let it out.

"How can you afford a night out like last night?" Cara asked.

"Don't ask questions you don't want answers to," Marie said. "I find a way to make ends meet, even if that means a little sacrificing here and there. Plus, the community feeds me more."

"The community hasn't been feeding you at all."

* * *

Cara returned to her little room above Eldorado that afternoon and planted face down in her bed. She let out a big sob and curled into the fetal position. She had been busy with the club, helping the Institute, and her relationship with Ada. She filled her time daily so she would not have to be alone with her thoughts. Yet, here she found herself, alone on her bed. The room seemed to shrink around her, the walls pressing in with a silent, suffocating weight. Her shadow stretched long and solitary across the floor in the dim light. She wrapped her arms around herself, a meager shield against the tide of memories that threatened to overwhelm her.

Molly's laughter echoed in her mind, a haunting reminder of the joy now lost. She could almost see her playing carefree, her smile a bright spark in a dark world. The void left by Catherine's death loomed large.

Each step in this foreign land felt heavy, her feet dragging as if mired in unseen quicksand. Words and phrases in a language she couldn't understand swirled around her, isolating her in a bubble of incomprehension.

In those moments, a cloud began to form in her mind. Her thoughts took over, telling her she was truly alone, adrift in a sea of unfamiliar faces and sounds, clinging to the fading echoes of a life once filled with warmth and connection. She was surrounded by accepting friends and family, so why did she feel this way?

Cara lay there until the sun set and darkness crept into her room. She didn't bother turning the lights on. She thought she might lay there for a while, letting the comfort of her bed swallow her. If she closed her eyes tightly, could she wish herself back home? She tried this and was still in her sewing room, staring at the machine that required a significant blood sacrifice.

It had been worth it to have Ada taking care of her, but now, Ada was history. Cara thought of how oblivious she had been. She had never expected someone who cared for her like that to betray her. She also felt stupid for dating a much older woman, which hadn't even crossed her mind.

She should have listened to Ronan, but surely she was old enough to decide who she loved. It was the first time she didn't have to feel ashamed for loving a woman, that perhaps she was blindsided by the idea of Ada and did not take the time to find out who she was. She was in love, or she thought she was. Now that love was gone.

Cara heard a gentle knock at the door and told whoever it was to go away. The door cracked open, and although she didn't see who it was, she instinctively knew it was Ronan.

He paused in the doorway for a moment. "It is so dark in here," he said.

"I like it like that. It feels like I'm in the caves by the sea. No one knows where I am, but they aren't worried," Cara said.

"I remember those vacations. Those were the good days," he said.

"Everything was less complicated then. I knew I was different. But I could hide with my thoughts. I could be a child," she said.

"You are a child. You are still learning. I don't know what role to play. I'm your big brother, Cara. I tried to be a father figure when I moved back home with you, but it was difficult as I was a boy myself. I know I overstepped when I saw you with Ada. I was fuming when I talked with Edith, but she told me you're

114

old enough to learn your own lessons. Ada's a great girl to work here, never misses a damn shift. But she is promiscuous and has her problems. She uses people like they're disposable, and you aren't the first one she's cast aside for something new and unique. Being here and being different in this community is all about figuring things out. When I arrived in Berlin, I did the same thing you did: I dove right in. I didn't know anything; I was paying boys for their company, drinking every day, and going to shows; it was all so thrilling. But over time, that sparkle wore off, and I was left with nothing, no money, no food, no pride, and a whole lot of grief from being kicked out of the family. I thought about going to seminary school," he said.

Cara chuckled at this.

He continued, "But then the community here did what it did best. The good people rallied around me, fed me, clothed me, and got me back on my feet. I got a small job here and started learning the ropes, and eventually, an opportunity came to run this place. Eldorado is magical. My dream is to have enough money to buy this place. But that's beside the point. I am not your father. I'm not your mother. And Lord knows I am not Gran. I want to be your brother, help you out, give you a soft place to fall. You can always come to me if you want to talk, but you must come to me."

Cara wiped the tears from her face and hugged Ronan. "It's hard to know who to trust," she admitted.

"Trust me. Trust your own blood," he replied.

Chapter 18

"You are looking positively depressed. It's getting on my nerves," Edith declared, walking into Cara's room. "Seriously, love cake, you need to move on. You had sex for a few weeks, and now you are lying in bed all depressed because she flirted with a Männin. I have an assignment for you. You are doing a photo shoot."

Edith's positivity was starting to anger Cara.

"I am not doing anything, Edith. I am staying in bed and never getting out again. I am the bed. I will never leave," she declared.

Edith ripped the sheets off the bed to reveal Cara curled tightly in a ball, hair nearly matted together, the stench of old sex on the sheets.

"Oh, for God's sake, Cara. You must wash the sheets. Get up." Edith dragged Cara by the arm out of bed and down the hallway to the communal bath she shared with Ronan and Edith. She found Marie there, in one of her best wigs, holding a scrub brush. She had a smile plastered on her face.

"What is happening?" Cara whined.

The women stripped her of her clothes and put her into the bathtub, scrubbing every crevice and corner they could find. Edith asked Marie if she could go into the sewing room and

116

take care of the smell. Marie nodded tenderly and left Edith and Cara in the tub. Cara began to cry.

"Ah!" Edith squawked.

Cara looked up at her, startled.

"Don't you dare cry. I'm done with the tears," she said.

Cara, surprised with herself, started to laugh.

"There she is, the lady we all love. Laughing," Edith said.

"I'm going crazy, Edith," Cara said, lines of mucus stretched across her salivating mouth.

Edith poured a bucket of warm water over Cara's head, wetting her hair and lathering up shampoo to clean it.

"You know, I can bathe myself," Cara said.

"Obviously, you cannot. You haven't for three weeks, darling."

Then, Marie burst through the door, holding her throat and gagging. "The sheets," she got out between a gag. She then began to dry heave and grabbed for the bucket.

"Marie, do you want the spotlight tonight? Are you Berlin's next best act? It's old sex smell. It's going to be a little fishy and a little funky, okay? Get over yourself. Honestly, these dolls want to be real women until they spend time with lesbians," Edith said.

She scrubbed hard into Cara's skull, removing all the dirt and built-up gunk on her scalp. She saw it floating around in white and brown bits in the bathwater. The next bucket of water was poured onto her head, and Edith wrung the water from her hair. She coated Brilliantine onto Cara's thick curls. It smelled rich and sweet; she had never smelled anything like it. She took the round product out of Edith's hands as she put it through her curls, pulling down strand by strand.

"What is this stuff? It's all in French," Cara asked.

117

"Don't worry about it, dear. It's what the gals use to make our hair look more, well, like yours," Edith replied.

Marie, now finished with dry heaving over the sink, took the Brilliantine out of Cara's hands and examined it.

"I've never heard of this," Marie exclaimed.

"It's everything. Believe me. Please take some and help me work through her locks. It's getting late," Edith said.

They let the thick grease stay on Cara's hair for a few minutes before shampooing again to get the grease out. It was quite the process, and all Cara did was sit there with her legs to her chest as the ladies of the night washed her hair. The water was warm but growing tepid the longer she sat in it, and her fingers were turning to mushy wrinkles. She held one up to Edith.

"Is this what a penis looks like?" she questioned.

Edith guffawed. "How would I know?" she remarked.

Marie looked at her sincerely. "You want to see one?" she whispered to her.

"Kind of," she said, "if you're offering," Cara said.

Then, Marie pulled up a floral skirt she was wearing and gently untucked her member from her knickers. It went down, all wrinkled, with a clean tip at the top. Cara slowly nodded her head.

"Oh," she remarked, "okay. Now I know. Thank you."

"Thank you?!" she screamed, "Honey, you are too much!" Marie tucked her member back into her knickers and lowered her skirt down.

"Now that's not what they all look like," Edith said.

"That is true. I had a Brit Milah," Marie said.

"What's a Brit Milah?" Cara asked.

"It's a Jewish ceremony where a baby boy is circumcised," Marie said, "I wish they took the entire damn thing off while

118

they were at it."

"I feel lucky enough to know Hirschfeld. He is going to help me out. Do you know some women I know want to keep theirs? I cannot imagine feeling that way," Edith said. "By the way, how is your stuff going with him?"

"Good. I'm making some surgery garments. He has particular fabrics he needs to use, and then I send them off as a sort of prototype. He then gets them produced somewhere else, but he likes to see what is possible before getting it mass-produced. It's complicated, and the garments need to be sanitized, that sort of thing. But I like doing it. I am also making garments for those thinking about transitioning but aren't ready to go through surgery yet. I made chest compressors. I tried one out on myself as a prototype, and it works well! I also made a wire bra that pushes your chest together. It looks like real cleavage; it's amazing! Edith, you wore that on stage the other night, didn't you?" she asked

"I sure did. And the money I got that night was unbelievable. That bra was magical," she said.

"And what else? Oh! He wanted me to create a flaccid penis to pee out of for those who want to stand and pee. But I don't know what material I would make that out of. I'm a seamstress, not a body architect. No material could harden like that. I haven't got a clue what I could make it out of," she said.

"Maybe you need to hang out with the Männin," Marie suggested, "I know a couple of them who would eat you up and give you all their secrets," she said, bopping her on the nose.

"I can't get involved with anyone again. My heart's been shattered," Cara replied, "I haven't felt this out of sorts since I left home."

"You can and you will," Edith said, scrubbing her hair gently.

119

"You know you both feel more like my family than my actual family," Cara said.

Marie put her hands on Cara's face and said, "We are honored to be your chosen family."

She kissed Cara gently on the forehead.

"You're going to make me cry," Edith said, slapping Marie gently on the arm.

She wiped tears from her eyes, "You are going to ruin your makeup!"

"Talk about something else!" Cara said.

"Your hair is almost done! Let's wrap you up in a towel. Marie, sweetheart, could you please grab a towel for this beauty's hair?" Edith asked.

After Cara dried off, they took her wrapped up in a towel down to the green room and got to work. Cara remembered hearing something about a photo shoot but didn't know what it meant. She was curious. "What is this whole thing about a photo shoot?" She yelled over the noise of the hair dryer.

Edith held her hand like a claw, scrunching up Cara's hair and wiggling the hair dryer back and forth so as not to burn her hand underneath. Cara was unsure what she was attempting to accomplish with this bizarre method of hair drying. Cara rarely dried her hair; there was no point. Edith seemed to know what she was doing.

"I can't hear you, darling. You need to wait," Edith said, turning off the hair dryer. "What did you say?"

The silence relieved Cara, who had the hairdryer pinned to her ear for a long while. "What is with the photo shoot? What are we doing all this for?"

Edith examined her hair. She started taking pomade and rubbing it in her hands, taking a strand of Cara's hair and twisting it around her fingers. She did that with a few sections as she talked. Her eyes were a beautiful dark brown with flecks of gold. Her lips always had lipstick on them, and Cara swore she had never seen those lips dry or cracked, even in the cold air of Berlin.

Cara knew Edith was from the United States, but she didn't talk much about it. She had an edge to her that Cara could not quite work out. Cara didn't know her whole story; she was always Edith, but Edith knew hers through Ronan. People didn't talk about their past lives much. Whenever Cara grew curious or tried to ask people about their time before the club, Ronan quickly pulled her into his office and educated her. Not everyone wants to reveal their past. They come to Berlin, places like Eldorado, to start a new life. Cara never asked Edith directly. However, she did ask how she learned to care for curls, how she got to Berlin, and how she knew to come to Eldorado.

"I'm not telling you the full details quite yet. Not until we get you all dolled up. Marie, could you please grab me that magical bra over there?" Edith smiled. "Imagine what this will do for your boobs!"

Cara narrowed her eyes and smiled back at her, "Edith, I need to send that off as a prototype eventually. I will make you another one."

"Not going to happen today, though. Put one of your boobs in this cup," she said, reaching underneath Cara's towel, "and then the other one in this one, and we smoosh together like this, et voila!"

Cara turned to look in the mirror to see herself with full, bolstered breasts covered by soft ultra-padded cups that pushed her boobs up and in. She dropped her towel to see

121

her reflection, a face full of make-up, soft curls drifting down near the small of her back, perfectly coiled and not a frizz to be seen on her head. She looked like a woman.

She put on a dress she had never seen before. It was low cut, and her breasts stood at attention against the soft fabric. It was black in the front, and the smooth satin fabric dipped in long triangles covering just enough of her breasts in the front. The back was completely open, and the dress fastened at the neck. The rest of the dress, the back that covered her butt, was white satin. Marie brought in long back gloves for her to wear and a sparkling necklace of emerald-like gems. She turned around and saw herself. She was in awe. Her reflection showed how she felt on the inside, now realized on the outside—all the years dressing other women to make them look beautiful meant everything to Cara. But now, it was her turn to shine. They led her onto the stage where a photographer stood in shiny black patent leather loafers, a suit fitted perfectly to her hips and waist, and a button-up buttoned just low enough for Cara to see her brassiere sticking out.

"This is Cara," Edith said to the photographer.

The photographer lit a cigarette. Her blonde hair was curled in buns underneath a cap. She wore pink lipstick and a light pink blush on her cheeks.

"Wow," she said, exhaling smoke. She's perfect," she said with a thick German accent. I don't speak much English, but I try my best, beautiful."

"Okay," Cara said nervously.

She was fidgeting with her gloves until Marie nudged her to stop.

The photographer spoke in German to Edith, who translated for Cara. She was shooting for *Die Freundin*. Cara's eyes grew large. Through clenched teeth, she told Edith that she remembered an issue about a woman riding naked on a horse and asked if she had to do that. Edith laughed heartily and said they would not be riding a horse today.

Then, the photographer, she found out her name was Emma, began to direct her with poses. The light would pop and flash as she held still for a few seconds. Edith and Marie had vanished, nowhere to be found, and suddenly Cara was alone with Emma. Emma walked over to her and fixed her hair a certain way, her blue eyes piercing through Cara. She picked up some of Cara's hair and draped them over her breasts. Then, without asking, she undid the clasp that fastened the halter together at the top and gently pulled it down to her waist. Then, she paused briefly, looking at Cara's wire bra contraption. Cara was so still that she had forgotten what she was wearing.

"Oh, I can, um –" she muttered.

"Do you mind?" Emma asked.

"No, not at all," Cara replied.

Emma gingerly pulled the wire bra contraption off Cara's breasts.

"A little small though?" Cara asked.

Emma looked at her breasts and asked, "May I? For artistic purposes?"

"Oh," Cara said, "yes."

Emma took each breast in her hand and thumbed over the nipples, sending shockwaves through Cara's body. Her breath hitched, and Emma began kissing her neck down to her breasts. She began to suck on Cara's pink nipples, switching between sucking on one and thumbing the other, leaving Cara squirming and holding onto Emma's head. She threw the hat off to reveal perfectly pinned buns. Emma reached down into

123

the dress to find that Cara was not wearing pants and that she was completely wet. They kissed as Emma started to go in and out, in and out, with her fingers, leaving Cara breathless. Cara was close to climaxing when Emma pulled out and commanded her to stay, just as she was. She fixed strands of Cara's hair and brushed her lipstick so it was slightly more symmetrical. Cara bit her finger to stave off the desire pulsing through her body and pushed her shoulder up to contort it.

"Perfect. Look into the camera," Emma commanded, "more like this, yes."

Cara caught her breath, and Emma finally declared that they were done. With that, Emma picked Cara up and carried her to her sewing room, where her bed was suspiciously made. Emma threw her on the bed, and they picked up exactly where they left off, with Emma's hand inside her.

A few years ago, she could have never imagined herself posing naked for a photographer, let alone having sex with a random stranger. When Emma was finished with her, Cara wanted to return. But Emma stopped and shook her head before leaving her bedroom.

Cara found herself breathless. These Berlin women were so forward with their sexuality, so unashamed. She was torn between feeling ashamed for what had happened and empowered whenever she had these encounters. It kept her tethered in who she was and who she wanted to become. She figured that one day she would figure it out, figure out what made her tick. Until then, she put on knickers and her casual day clothes and went downstairs to assess how much clothing needed to be cleared off the stage. She guessed it couldn't be too bad. She went downstairs to see Emma with Marie and Edith.

"You don't have to pay me to do that, you know," Emma said, waving her hand.

"Then we'll take the money back," Edith said.

Emma paused and changed the subject.

"She is going to be the most beautiful woman on the cover. These will be flying off the shelf."

Cara smiled and knew Edith and Marie paid Emma extra, but it didn't matter because her friends paid for her to get over someone who didn't matter anyway. Maybe this was how she would get over all her problems, to be wholly destitute and be everything Gran warned her about. Even a Llangollen woman wouldn't dare to pay someone to have sex with them.

III

Part Three

Downfall of the Weimar Republic
1933

Chapter 19

The memory of the photo shoot hung framed on her bedroom wall, the ink slightly washed out and its edges yellowing from years of direct sunlight. A handwritten translation was tucked in behind the frame courtesy of Marie. Cara was featured on the cover as "Lesbische Modedesignerin" or Lesbian Fashion Designer. The exposure had been great for Cara's business, and the years following the release of that issue had been a mad rush of keeping up with requests, working with the Institute, and managing backstage at Eldorado. Cara wished there were two of her, and due to her workload, the only people she saw were Edith, Marie, and Ronan. Women came and went. She stopped feeling guilty about these quick encounters. Her confidence grew in the art of seduction. However, no one seemed to stick around for long, and Cara was okay with that. Her work was more important. When she felt like she could finally get her head above water, she slowly started to lose business.

It started when Ronan asked Cara to be backstage for four nights instead of six. Fewer customers were coming into the club, so he decided to only open on the busiest days to keep costs down. Then, Dr. Hirschfeld stopped requesting surgical garment prototypes, saying fewer clients were interested in transition surgery.

These two requests didn't worry her initially, as she still had plenty of fittings and wardrobe requests to fulfill. But she did begin to worry when Ronan announced Eldorado could only afford to be open two days per week. Then, Magnus disappeared, and no one had heard from him in weeks. The Institute remained open, but she did not go inside without him there. The requests for fittings went from being rescheduled to fully canceled. The final death knell: no work, no requests, and the club was closed. This was, unfortunately, one of those days.

She sat in her bed, tossed a ball of yarn in the air, and caught it repeatedly. Her stomach growled, and she thought about brewing extra strong coffee and brushing up on her German by reading the newspaper. Although she had been in Germany for years, most people spoke English with her, as their English was better than her German. She mostly used her German to stay current on the political tensions in Germany.

Adolf Hitler was growing in popularity among the people. The country's economic divide grew more expansive by the day, and the German people wanted answers. Hitler promised to restore the country to its former prosperous state. He also gave the people a place to point a finger at the current economic devastation. He blamed the Jews not only for the German's loss in the first war but also for the current class divide.

Cara read *Mein Kampf*. She read nothing particularly notable in it. Hitler's ideas, in their purest form, were far from original, yet when he spoke, it was as if those ideas were fresh, magical resolutions. He could hypnotize a crowd and have them jeering, shouting, and signaling along with him. Everywhere he spoke, he gained more devoted disciples.

Cara listened to his speeches on the radio, and what caught her attention was his desire to have a purely Aryan race. When Cara first heard this, he would briefly mention this idea as soft launching it before it could land. However, as times were getting more challenging in Berlin with the fall of the Weimar Republic, and with him encouraging the notion that Jews were to blame, this dangerous idea was gaining more power.

She tossed the ball of yarn up in the air, and the ball hit her face. She resigned and stared up at the ceiling, a large crack forming under the dried puddles of rain that looked like blooms of milky tea. She sighed. Tomorrow, the club would be open. Tomorrow, she could be backstage.

A few members of Hitler's military organization frequented Eldorado and weren't exactly discreet about their desires. Edith had been seeing a member as a floor girl, one of Hitler's confidants, who told her that Hitler was generally okay with homosexuality so long as it didn't interfere with his party or what he wanted to accomplish. So, more of them came in.

They called themselves the Sturmabteilung or Storm Division.

Edith and Cara had discussed the organization in detail, and Cara was conflicted about how she felt about them coming into the club. If Hitler was okay with homosexuality, then they had nothing to worry about. However, the more attention he received, the bolder he was in his claims of creating a better society, one where there was no more poverty, better roads, cars, and all things the community could see working for them. On the other hand, whenever there was an anti-Jewish statement or when he said he wanted to restore Germany to its golden days, Cara got queasy. The members who came to Eldorado were kind, treated the staff well, and paid a lot to be

131

there. The members of the Storm Division gave the floor girls extra money. Cara thought about working the floor with Edith and Marie, as her savings were dwindling. With this thought, she got out of bed and went into the hallway to make herself coffee. However, when she did, she heard muffled sobs coming out of Ronan's office.

She listened outside and peeked through the small opening of the door to see his head in Edith's lap, and she stroked the back of his neck with her long dark fingers and chipped red fingernail polish. His books were open to a page with a large red circle on a fast encroaching date, the beginning of the New Year. He overheard Edith telling him it would be okay and that he had done his best. He cried out that he had let everyone down, but Edith reminded him that if not for him, the folks at Eldorado would be far worse off than they were now. She promised them they would figure out how to let the workers know and that they could not fault him for his efforts. How could he know, she said, that there would be these unprecedented times? The club was roaring only a couple of years ago and was successful financially. He had saved and scraped, and this is where they were. He began to cry even harder.

Cara quietly snuck past the office and down the stairs of the club. Instead of going to the galley kitchen, she walked out of the heavy doors. The frigid air made her cheeks sting. She had gone outside without a coat but was on a mission. She marched down to her local newspaper station. When she arrived, she swung the door open and immediately placed two Deutsche marks on the receptionist's desk.

"I'd like to place an advertisement in the paper," she said.

132

* * *

The following week, a man responded to her advertisement. She sold her sewing machine to him, an aristocrat, who wanted to buy his wife something for the holidays. He explained they were also trying to be careful with money, so that was why he was buying the machine second-hand. She ensured Ronan was out when the gentleman picked it up with friends. She stuffed the paper Deutsche mark in an envelope and put it on Ronan's desk. The costumes she used to produce were now being used regularly. She did not need a sewing machine. They had to make do with what they had. When Ronan found the envelope, he rushed into Cara's room to see her hand sewing a torn zipper for the performance that night.

"Cara, what is this?" he asked her indignantly.

Cara shrugged her shoulders, "I don't need it like I used to, Ro. It's not much money in terms of running the club, but it's a little extra cushion if you need it. Promise me you'll put that toward savings," she said, not even looking up from her sewing.

Ronan hugged her from behind. Cara wriggled out of the hug and looked at him directly. The once bright glowing eyes were bloodshot like he hadn't slept in a few days.

"Aw, Ro, you look horrible," Cara said bluntly.

"Thanks. I appreciate your honesty," he retorted.

"I'm sorry. It's just, I meant—"

"Don't worry about it. Well, with your help, we may be able to put off closing the club down until after the holidays. Anyway, we don't have much we can do for Christmas. Is there anything you want to do?"

Chapter 20

The following Sunday before Christmas, Marie and Cara went for a walk. It was freezing that day, and the wind had picked up through the streets, blowing about the smell of garbage. Berlin had returned to its original smelly state, which had been ousted not so long ago, with the installation of the sewer system. Now, they were smelling the sewage of the poor without a place to go to the toilet beside the street.

"You've been looking sad, dear," Marie noted. She was unusually attuned to Cara's emotions.

"I've been feeling uncertain of my future. It reminds me of when I was a little girl, trying to find stability and eventually making it on my own. Times are so strange right now. I sold my sewing machine, and I wanted to do that to help Ronan. But it was like it was a sign. When the men came to pick up the machine, I saw bits of my dried blood from when I accidentally sewed my finger. It reminded me of the blood I shed for this place, the sacrifices I made to be here and live freely," Cara said.

Marie paused. "You feel uncertain and unsettled," she said.

"Yes, you could say that. The strange thing is when I used to feel this way, I knew that at some point, I'd be going to church. Even though I've had a complicated relationship with the church, I still used to find peace in hearing the church bells, the ritual of speaking Latin, and the comfort of knowing that no matter where I am in the world, it will be the same—even placing my hand in the oily holy water, where there have been numerous hands just like mine, and blessing myself with the sign of the cross like everyone who has come before me. I miss genuflecting before entering a pew or singing hymns that bring such a comforting message that I do not need to be afraid because something greater than me has a plan. Going from hearing this message, along with the other horrible ones, don't get me wrong, the damnation and the hell and the guilt are very real, too. I have been busy these past few years. Now that I am slowing down, it feels like something is missing. I don't know if I believe in a God. I can't find peace with it, and I can't find peace without it. It's part of who I am and how I grew up. It sounds ridiculous," she said, "but I miss the bells."

Marie looped her arm through Cara's and stroked it gently. "I can understand that. You miss the peace of mind of believing in something greater than yourself. There's nothing foolish in that. You can still believe in something greater than yourself, even if it is not a God. And what the Church represents is complicated. The world is not black and white; it's many shades of gray. Those who believe otherwise lead a life of blissful ignorance," Marie said, "and we know too much to live in ignorance."

"Yes, I guess so," Cara said, sniffling.

"Oh dear, don't cry over a half-naked man on a piece of wood. You can still go to church. You won't spontaneously combust upon entering, you know," Marie said.

"The holidays always bring up more feelings. I want so desperately to go home but cannot afford to. My family has likely forgotten about me and moved on with their lives. Yet, I miss Ireland. I miss my home. I didn't want to leave, but I felt I had no choice. I should be happy I'm in paradise. I don't have to wake up to go to mass or deal with the gossip and the stigma of being different. However, I feel like I was ripped away, and I haven't felt the same since," Cara admitted.

They continued their walk, turning the corner and ending where they began. They looked at each other, nodded, and continued for another loop around the block. They stopped at the newspaper stand that had another headline about Adolf Hitler and his speech. Cara decided to spend some of her money on a paper, as she liked to stay current on what was happening with the Hitler hysteria. She rolled up the newspaper and tucked it under her arm.

"This Hitler is scaring me," Cara said discreetly.

"Why are you speaking so low?" Marie queried. "He doesn't scare me. With the amount of money I make from his members and the times I've had with them, I mean, hot damn, honey! I think he is for the average Volk. He's progressive."

"Progressive?" Cara asked, "Doesn't he want to return to Germany as it was in the past?"

"Yes, but he's also promising to get us out of poverty, build a road system, make new jobs, get us more land. Get rid of the Treaty of Versailles. Can you imagine us being paid more, having more people come into the club, and restoring it to how it was when we first met? Remember that, Cara? That's what he's promising," Marie said. "He's such a mesmerizing speaker. So handsome, too."

"Marie, but what about the whole Aryan race thing? He alluded to a lot of the problems being because of the Jewish population," she said.

"Well, look at who is doing well in the 'Great Depression'. It's the Jews. They have all the money," Marie said.

"That's a generalization, though, and not necessarily true. Sure, some Jewish people have wealth, but it's not every Jewish person," Cara said.

"Look, all I'm saying is, hear him speak a little more. He blames Jewish people only occasionally. Everything else he says, like restoring Germany to a time when we had more land or when there was more tradition, are the concepts to hold onto. Times were simpler then, Cara. You wouldn't know. You weren't even a twinkle in your mother's eye. As a much older woman, I am telling you that I think Hitler could be good for Germany. Plus, you know all the burned butter we've received over the years?"

"Yes?" Cara questioned.

"It's because the Jews in this town can afford fresh butter. The restaurants reuse the butter for us lowly occasional guests. So selfish," Marie said.

Cara shook her head, "That doesn't make any sense."

"The Jews bring in butter into the restaurants around here— their own personal supply. The restaurants reuse the butter if we ask for it because it's all they have. I know this because I'm friends with Friedrich; he tells me everything about the Jews," Marie said confidently.

"Aren't you Jewish?" Cara asked

"My mother was Jewish," Marie responded.

They rounded another corner and went their separate ways, a silence growing between them. Marie walked back to her flat, and Cara returned to her sewing room, where she would continue throwing a ball of yarn into the air and catching it until it was time for dinner: a slice of dense rye bread with cheese, potatoes, and cabbage.

* * *

On Christmas morning, Ronan woke Cara up at six and told her to get dressed. She shook her head and looked outside, as it was still dark and cloudy and cold.

"We aren't doing gifts this year, Ro. I want to go back to sleep. I had some of the well-liquor last night. I feel horrible," she said.

"Cara, I promise it will be worth it. Come on. Get dressed. Marie is waiting for us downstairs."

Cara peeled her eyes open and got dressed in the dark. She went downstairs into the club's belly to find Marie and Ronan sitting down at a table, waiting for her. During the day, she rarely came downstairs except to brew coffee. Seeing it now without crowds, she noticed the cobwebs in the ceiling and the dust piles collecting in the corners of the floorboards. The table where Marie and Ronan sat was heavily scratched and chipped. One of the legs was short, and it wobbled as they stood.

"We have a surprise for you! Put on your coat; we're going out," Marie said.

They all put on their coats, and Cara followed suit, groaning about how early it was on Christmas morning to have a surprise.

They went outside and walked for a bit until they arrived at a cathedral. It had a large green dome with a cross on top, large columns, and depictions of Christ on the cross and angels carved into the stone. They arrived just in time to hear the bells toll and saw people walk into the church, opening the

138

large glass doors to the warm and inviting service. Cara let out a breath.

"I don't know how I feel," she said.

"I don't either. But I imagine we feel similarly. The only way to know is to go in. If we don't spontaneously catch fire, I think we are okay to participate," Ronan said, "It's only Christmas mass. We've sat through far worse."

The three looped arm-in-arm and walked up the stone steps into St. Hedwig's for Christmas mass as if preparing to walk into battle. Yet, the church was warm and smelled of sweet incense, and they gratefully took off their coats upon entering. Cara's shoulders relaxed; she dipped her fingers into the golden bowl of holy water and made the sign of the cross. Marie stared intently at her, and Cara realized that Marie had never been to a Catholic service.

"Oh, so dip your hands in here," she told her, "And then put it on your forehead, chest, left shoulder, right. There you go," she said.

They chose a pew in the back, and Ronan and Cara discussed whether they should take communion. The consensus was they would go up to the altar with their arms crossed and get a blessing. They hadn't been to confession in quite some time, and both leading semi-debaucherous lifestyles, they didn't see why they should interfere when they hadn't been to mass in so long. Although there would be no harm in taking communion, the rituals and traditions were still deeply ingrained in them. Ronan suggested leaving after communion, but Cara argued with him that they would be like those Catholics who went to holiday mass once per year and left before the rush. Ronan looked at her with narrowed eyes.

"Isn't that exactly what we are?" he asked.

"I guess you're right. Let's figure it out as we go along," Cara said.

The mass was typical, except for the homily. At first, the priest talked about Christmas and the birth of Jesus. This led to references the priest made to unprecedented times and the rise of hatred toward Jewish people. He was outspoken during this homily against this hatred and invited a local rabbi to stand.

"The Catholic church stands beside our Jewish brothers and sisters. Anyone who preaches genocide as a remedy to economic downfall is not a true believer in God."

He then asked the rabbi to sit.

"I would have thought that the Catholics would be pro-Hitler," Marie whispered.

"The church cannot be for or against anything political. They can only state the church's values," Cara explained. She wished the church would stand with the Schwul. Her stomach tightened. Although Hitler's cronies patronized elDorado, the political cartoons she read in the newspapers were developing into bold and crass remarks about his division's weakness. Being a Schwul meant being a lesser man. Although it was meant to make light of the political situation and continue the Weimar Republic, Cara felt it would eventually backfire if Hitler came to power.

When it came time for communion, Cara, Ronan, and Marie decided to leave instead of taking a blessing. They made their way toward the exit until, out of the corner of Cara's eye, she saw the chapel was open. She suggested they light some candles before leaving, before also spotting the rectory.

"Ro, I bet there's some communion wine in there. Molly and I used to steal some from the church. Should we grab some?

We'd have some for Christmas!" Cara asked.

"Good joke, Cara," he replied.

"I won't get caught," she whispered.

"We must go back and start cooking. Come on, let's get going," he replied sharply.

"I'll catch up with you later," she whispered loudly.

Ronan's eyes grew large, and he started shifting his weight from side to side as if trying to decide to go toward Cara or the exit.

He mumbled, "I am not her parent," while Cara waved goodbye. Slowly, she walked backward, waiting to see if Ronan or Marie would join her.

"I'm not going with her," Marie said, flipping her hair over her shoulder. She put her coat on and buttoned it, a custom coat that Cara made with a cinched waist to accentuate her figure. Ronan stood there, forehead sweating, but it was too late. Cara had gone toward the rectory, opened the door, and walked right in.

"She seems so boring, and then suddenly...," Marie said, flustered, "I'm not a part of this. I'm already collecting looks. I barely had time to shave today. I'm going outside and walking back to Eldorado."

Off Marie went, out the doors, into the cold, bitter December air.

When Cara entered the rectory, she first passed a large kitchen, where a gentleman stopped her.

"May I help you, my child?"

"Excuse me. I was sent by my son, one of the altar boys. You see, they ran out of communion wine at mass, and he asked me to fetch some for the next one," she said confidently.

The man looked at her through narrowed eyes, sizing her

up. He didn't look like a priest. He wore gray suit trousers and a button-up shirt, and Cara caught him making coffee that looked like mud. Then, she recognized him.

He frequented Eldorado, one of the supposed priests of St. Hedwig's. His forehead started sweating, and he fidgeted with the coffee pot. He took a mug from one of the cabinets, and it fumbled out of his hand. It landed on the floor, thankfully unbroken. Cara picked it up and handed it to him with a half-awkward smile.

"Don't say anything," he said, "I'll give you whatever you want," he said under his breath.

Cara saw his face drain of color. It was not her intention to go in and frighten someone like this. "I won't say anything. I'm sorry. All I want is some communion wine for the feast tonight. Unconsecrated, of course." She started twirling her hair, waiting for his next move.

He held up a finger and walked around her.

She waited there momentarily, and he returned with two giant jugs of communion wine. "Thank you," she whispered, "I'm sorry. I didn't mean to make you feel caught –"

"Please leave," he begged.

"Are you coming tonight? Free wine!" She tried to get a laugh out of him to no avail.

"No, I'm not coming tonight," he whispered harshly. He paused, "Okay, maybe. I don't know. Just get out of here, go go go go go!" He gained more confidence to push her on the back and usher her out the door.

She left through the same door she entered, back through the church, and out the front steps of St. Hedwig's with the communion wine. She saw Ronan outside, pacing back and forth at the bottom of the large stone staircase. When he looked up and saw Cara, she held up the two giant jugs in celebration. "Let's go get smashed!" she yelled.

"Shut up, and let's go, now," he scolded her, took her arm harshly, and walked swiftly toward Eldorado.

"Lighten up, Ronan," she puffed, "It's just a little wine. Plus, I saw one of our regulars there," she said.

Ronan was silent and continued pulling Cara along briskly, with Cara almost running to keep up with him. By the time they were out of the neighborhood of St. Hedwig's and entered their own, Cara pulled Ronan back with what she could, and she hooked one elbow in his. She set down the jugs of wine and grabbed Ronan by the shoulders.

"Why are you so upset? It's a little wine. We'll share it," she said.

"We are not the only people who are going without, Cara. Stealing from the church? I understand you've changed, but we aren't the only ones affected right now."

"St. Hedwig's has plenty of gold trimmings. I think they will survive without their wine," Cara replied.

Chapter 21

When they returned to Eldorado, things started to stir around the club. The community of workers and their chosen families had come to start Christmas breakfast. The staff smiled, sang Christmas carols, and laughed over coffee and pastries. Although the site was warm, Cara was feeling cold. When Ronan walked in red in the face, the staff grew quiet and curious, asking him what was wrong. All he could manage to say was, "Enjoy the wine." Cara slammed the two jugs of wine on the table, making Edith and Ronan jump. She followed them both up the stairs, stomping all the way up. Edith and Ronan slammed the door in her face when they got to the office.

Cara lost her temper. "You two are loo-lah!" she shouted.

The entire club heard. Just then, the door swung open, and it was Edith, wearing a stern expression that made Cara numb. She did not raise her voice. "You've done enough for today, Cara. Why don't you be a kleptomaniac in another part of town because you are no longer welcome here." She slammed the door in her face again.

Cara defeated, stomped her way down the stairs, grabbed both jugs of communion wine, and went to a nearby park. She sat on a bench, cracked open one of the jugs, and started taking swigs. She wrapped herself tightly with her coat and lay on a bench, desperately wanting to fall asleep. It wasn't her idea in the first place to go to mass. She had wanted to continue sleeping. Bells were not worth this much trouble.

She drifted in and out of consciousness and dreamt of flying.

Someone cut her wings, and she landed in an all-white room on the floor. There was no beginning and no end. She looked down to feel the floor, but it had no tactile feel or temperature. It felt like nothing. Suddenly, a woman appeared before her. She was utterly ethereal with long, curly brown hair and an unwrinkled face, dressed in a white garment tied with a white rope. At first, it looked like a female Jesus standing before her, looking lovingly down at her. When Cara looked into the woman's eyes, she realized it was Catherine. Catherine without wrinkles. Catherine with neat curls. Catherine with a smile. They embraced. Cara didn't speak but wept in her arms. It had been four years since the funeral and four years since she'd seen a face from home.

Catherine let her go and gently took her hand. They walked into the infinite space together in silence. Neither of them spoke, but they seemed to communicate through memories. Catherine emanated a warm glow. It was as if Cara was suffocating, desperate for air on the park bench not even a moment ago, and when she awoke to Catherine, she was gasping for air, filling her lungs with precious oxygen.

She was wobbly walking next to a goddess like Catherine, who didn't notice. Like a movie, Cara looked into the infinite space. She saw her memories projected onto them: she and Molly were embracing as children and laughing together, Molly's little blonde ringlets bouncing in her face. It was summer holidays on the coast, and they ran around in the sand in their swimsuits outside in the bright sun. Catherine bought them oversized sunglasses, and they

145

spent the entire summer wearing them and kissing each other on both cheeks. They thought they were the height of sophistication. Cara looked at the beach towels in the movie memory, the salmon-striped white ones she would be wrapped up in as her dad carried her flopping, sleeping, toddler body back to their rented vacation house. It was the only time she remembered her father going with the family on a vacation, and she cherished the memory of him caring for her.

The following projection to her right showed her and Molly playing dress up with Catherine's clothes, in high heels that looked like submarine ships on their tiny feet, and wearing Catherine's rouge, which smelled like dusty mothballs. They danced around the living room, giving their parents a performance. Molly had helped her sew a set of rags into two dresses they wore during the performance. They draped themselves in costume jewelry, borrowed their neighbors' Cabrioles, and stuffed the ends with talcum powder, thinking it would look like smoke when exhaled.

However, she and Molly did not practice this theory and decided to put it to the test during their performance. During the performance, they both exhaled on the Cabrioles at the same time. They packed the Cabrioles so tightly that they were exhaling for a few seconds, their cheeks puffing out with stretched skin and increased pressure before the packed powder exploded out in a pellet, and when it landed, it left a scattered pile of powder on the floor. She watched her and Molly's panicked faces on the projection, nervous that they would get in trouble and seeing the relief wash over them as their mothers started crying with laughter, clutching their stomachs, slapping their knees, and gasping for air. She had never seen her mother laugh so hard. Cara's smile grew wide at this memory, and when she looked up at Catherine, she saw she was smiling too.

They walked on from this memory to the next projection of her and

Molly gazing into each other's eyes, a flask of whiskey between them on a grassy knoll. Cara knew what was coming next, and she started to sweat, looking at Catherine, who continued watching the movie, her hand over her heart, smiling. They watched as Molly looked into Cara's eyes and kissed her; both were seventeen, so carefree and rebellious. That kiss had confirmed what Cara had long suspected: that she was different.

Her heart began to ache for that memory, and she looked on as she cupped Molly's face and separated their soft lips. Later, she collapsed on the long grass, Molly's head on her chest, breathing together slowly and deeply as the sun set. Cara attempted to separate from Catherine and walk into the memory, but Catherine still held Cara's hand and stood firm, stopping her from stepping into the past.

They continued. The space turned white again, and Cara attempted to open her mouth to speak, but her breath would hitch and catch in her throat, an unseen force maintaining the silence. Cara tried to walk in front of Catherine, to put up her hands as if to say "stop," but no matter how she tried to command her movement, it was like walking through thick clay, and Catherine maintained their slow and steady pace until she stopped. Catherine looked down at her, and when she opened her mouth, it was as if her voice was projecting all around the infinite space and even in Cara's head.

"Go home."

Cara tried to reason with her, stop her, and explain that she was not welcome home. Germany was her home, and even if things were hard with Ronan, they would patch things up. Plus, what kind of life would she live if she had to go back home? Catherine shook her head. Even though Cara did not state these things, she seemed to understand. Tears started falling out of Catherine's eyes, and she opened her mouth again.

147

"Go home," the room echoed. " Go home, go home, go home, go home, go home, go home."

Finally, Cara felt whatever force was holding her mouth closed had loosened. "Why?" she asked, exasperated.

Catherine clutched her chest, her entire body filled with tremors, as she collapsed onto the floor. When she entered this realm, the relaxed face Cara saw was now paralyzed, frozen. Cara knelt and tilted Catherine's face so she could look into her eyes. Her eyes were playing a movie, and her once-dark pupils were now screening, but Cara couldn't determine what was happening. She got closer to Catherine's eyes, their pupils together, to see what was happening. Their eyes touched, and the harder she pressed, the further she fell into the memory. She retreated briefly, looking at Catherine staring up into infinity, until Catherine grabbed Cara by the neck with such force that Cara started choking, and she pulled her into her face, immersing her into a different world.

Cara landed on a semi-familiar street where Eldorado was located, but it was deserted. She heard the roar of warplanes overhead, and from their release, she could see fast-approaching life-size sewing needles, sharp and aimed at her head. She ran as fast as she could away from the impending doom, as one needle impaled a tree, splitting it in half. More warplanes flew overhead, and the once deserted street was suddenly full of people she knew from the club and people she knew from being around Berlin, who she bumped into frequently at grocery stores, the Institute, and doctor's offices. She flailed her arms, trying to warn them of the warplanes overhead, dropping large sewing needles, but they didn't see or hear her. The planes dropped more needles, one impaling Edith through the head, popping out bits of blood and brain onto the street, and it continued to rain needles all over the people, puncturing them, splitting their flesh apart. Cara heard their shrieks and their screams, and the *entire street was filled with blood. The sun raged hot, and the whole street stank of rotting bodies. They were all left there as time sped up, no one coming to clean up the disaster until a large tank came that had a scoop on the end of it, scooping up the dead bodies and putting them into a massive hole, continuing with its journey as far as Cara could see.*

She looked to the sky, blue, clear, and cloudless, and shouted into the void, wanting something to hit her, have her be impaled too, be gone. There was nothing. Nothing came for her, just blue skies and sun shining on a deserted Berlin street, blood staining the pavement. She wanted to get out of this reality and back to the safety of Catherine and the infinite space. She found a black hole above her, and she jumped up to clutch her hands on the edge and pull herself up and out of Catherine's pupil.

She woke up on the park bench, right where she dozed off; half a glass jug of wine was gone, the other still full, just as she left it. The sun was high, midday, and the park was still eerily deserted, even for Christmas morning. No children were on swings or slides, no groups of people celebrating together, no carolers, just cold, dead silence. Cara loosened her coat buttons and blinked away the blurred sleep from her eyes. She wore a dazed expression as if attempting to discern reality from fiction. Cara stood up and journeyed, lugging the jugs of wine back toward Eldorado. When she arrived at the club, she shifted one of the jugs onto her left hip, holding it carefully while attempting to open one of the doors. Swinging it open, she saw the club was deserted. Everyone who had arrived for the Christmas party vanished. Usually, even on days off, a few performers would mark their sets, working with lights and a director to assemble everything. The silence grew, and she ached for the clicking sound of her sewing

149

machine, methodically going over the material needed for the performances. Her heart sank. A tiny sliver of light came in through one of the windows, dust dancing in the ray. The wind blew against the panes, finding holes to howl through. Cara heard the sharp cracks of the settling building and the creaking of footsteps upstairs. She took a deep breath and headed up.

Cara and Ronan locked eyes before she made it up the stairs.

"Hi," she said, finally reaching the top.

"Hi. Let's go into my office," he suggested.

They settled in together, each on different wooden chairs. Cara rarely sat down in the office anymore. She took a closer inventory of what Ronan had on his desk: a photo of their mother she had never seen before, her hair in a chiffon bun and button-up blouse, piles of papers with big round stamps that read "invoice overdue," and a small, cleared space in the exact shape of a square, where there was an actual wooden desk underneath.

"Cara, I'm sorry. Everything has been so stressful with the club. I haven't slept in quite some time. I overreacted. I do feel like I'm going crazy. I am starting to see things, to hear things that aren't there. I don't know what to do."

Cara put her hand on Ronan's.

"You and I ran away from Dublin and worked at a perverted club. Sometimes, I become so overwhelmed with the guilt and shame of it all, like this business is failing because I fell from God. God is punishing me," he said.

"This isn't a perverted club. This is a community you've helped to create. You have no idea what this means to me, what this place means to all of us," she said.

"And how the community I've created can't keep its doors open past January," he choked out a sob.

"We'll find a way. Even if it's not Eldorado, we'll find a way to stay together. You and I are family. We're blood," she said, rubbing his arm.

"I canceled Christmas," he said. We need the money to stay open, and I can't feed the community when I can't even feed myself," he got out.

Cara noticed how frail he had become. His bones were protruding from his hands, and his once muscular figure was nothing but skin on bone. His cheeks were sunken and sallow, and his trousers collected material at the top. His belt was looped around a time and a half, cinching the fabric as close to his body as possible.

"We will get you some food, Ronan," Cara said.

"Even if I wanted to eat, I couldn't. I'm such a mess. I wanted to buy this place, but it's all shot to hell. This is God's punishment for me: to run a successful business and have the rug pulled out from under me. I don't understand; I thought I was a good person," he rambled.

"You are a good person, Ro. God is not punishing you. We are in the middle of an economic hardship. You aren't the only one feeling this way. Talk to some other business owners," she suggested.

He rolled his eyes at her and scoffed, "Sure, I'll go talk to other business owners about how my perverted club is failing. That will go very well."

She took a deep breath at the snarky comment, "Ronan, there are other clubs in this neighborhood far more perverted than Eldorado. You know there are. Talk to the other owners; it may make you feel less alone about what you are going through. I can help you only so much. I'm here for you," she said.

Ronan wiped away his tears and blew into his handkerchief

151

he pulled from his back pocket.

"Ro?" she asked inquisitively.

"Yes?"

"Do you believe in ghosts?"

* * *

Christmas really was canceled. No one was at the club, so she took this as an opportunity for her and Ronan to bond. They drank until no more communion wine was left in the glass jug. She was surprised how little she and Ronan communicated over the years except in passing. Ronan told her that she thought the visit from Catherine was real and that she should believe and count it as a visit. However, he was perplexed as to why she would tell her to get out and said that sewing needles impaling people was only a dream she could have.

"No one else could have a nightmare about sewing needles," he told her, following him saying how ludicrous of a dream it was.

Cara told him she couldn't shake the feeling that Catherine had told her to go home. It was what was bothering her the most.

"Dreams are just that, Cara, dreams," Ronan said.

"You don't understand. It felt so real," Cara said.

"I do believe it was Catherine. But I don't think you should read into her asking to go through her eyeball or that sewing needles will fall from the sky soon. That's an oddity of the mind. Don't worry so much about it. You are stressed, and the stress has transferred to your dreams. That's all it means."

Chapter 22

New Year's Eve was the last time the club was to be open. There was a whole party planned for its closing. Any money Ronan had left over was used to refill the liquor bottles with actual liquor. He *had* been refilling them with water to make them last longer. Cara had a short break between Christmas and New Year's to make the costumes look as bright as they did when she first created them. They invited back old performers who had quit for one reason or another. Current performers were excited to share the stage one last time. Everyone seemed to be there, including a few members of the Sturmabteilung, who called themselves SAs. It made Cara a little nervous to have members of the SA at the club in the first place.

The club was packed and gleaming as if it were the old days. The tables were fixed and sturdy, the cobwebs swept, and not a speck of dust was to be found. The club looked nearly identical to when Cara first arrived in Berlin. As a nod to her first arrival, Cara wore the silver beaded tank dress she had in her wardrobe. It was stunning, and when she had a moment alone, she found herself swishing her hips back and forth to make the dress dance. Cara was backstage, fixing costumes and dressing performers. Then, Edith came back breathing heavily, having performed her heart out on stage as if for the last time.

"I sang that for the cute SA right over there," she pointed at him.

He had a Wehrmacht symbol on his uniform.

"I still can't believe they hang out here with all the political cartoons circulating about certain members being caught here," Cara said.

"Oh, I know. But they all have a private life. And what's private is private. But I do know a few secrets," Edith giggled.

"Secrets? What kind of secrets?" Cara urged on.

"Well, I can't say otherwise. They wouldn't be secrets, darling. And I need to get paid. So, I will keep those secrets," Edith replied.

Cara couldn't help but wonder if she was safe here. She was unsure as long as the SAs continued to come to the club. It wasn't like they did anything in particular. They drank, paid for the company, and seemed delighted by the shows. After all, they were humans. All humans have urges and itches they need to scratch. Still, Cara felt a drop in the pit of her stomach, and she couldn't shake the feeling that as long as they continued to come in and patronize the bar, there would always be eyes on the community.

"At what cost, Edith?" Cara finally replied.

Edith rolled her eyes.

"You are worried about nothing. It's not us they want. You know how many SAs have rolled into Eldorado —" Edith replied.

"That's exactly what I'm concerned about," Cara kept her voice low. There are rumors of returning to an earlier lifestyle in Germany, which includes upholding the ban."

"We've got around that for thirty years, plus we're closing

after tonight. Why start worrying now? Calm down. Get yourself a drink, sew something. You are making me sad," Edith said.

She stormed off toward the green room, and Ronan, having walked into this tense situation, looked puzzled.

"Is she okay?" he asked.

"She's entertaining members of the SA. I don't know, Ro. You know how unsure I am about this. Why would we be going back to make Germany a restored promised land when that's exactly when they made us illegal? I do not believe that this will last forever," she said.

"Cara, the SAs are the reason we could throw a final party tonight. Those men single-handedly are keeping the club open. I get where you're coming from, but if SA members are willing to be seen here, at Eldorado, I don't think we have anything to worry about," he said. "I think the SA is progressive enough to allow those cartoons to pass in the newspapers about their own coming here. It's the 30's! People are poor, but we're here and celebrating while we can. They are with the times. I'm not worried, and they pay well. Leave Edith alone."

Cara pursed her lips and said nothing more on the topic. She came out for the champagne toast and apologized to Edith, and they clinked glasses together. Afterward, they discussed the Weimar Republic.

"I understand Hitler's been arrested before. You must understand, Cara, that the Weimar Republic has allowed us to get into this impoverished state in the first place. The Republic is why our club is closing. The man is passionate, but who wouldn't be about his own country? I think he's going to fix things; he's promising new jobs to restore Germany to get rid of the Treaty of Versailles, which is sucking our country dry.

155

Come, meet an SA, dear," she said, leading her over to a table full of uniformed men.

"Hi, boys. This is our seamstress from the Emerald Isle, Cara. Cara, these are the SA men," she said.

One of the SA men clapped his hands on his lap, and Edith followed dutifully and sat on his lap, putting her arms around his neck.

"You are too cute," she cooed.

"My lap is open, dear," one of the men said.

"Oh, I–" Cara stumbled, nervously folding her napkin into a tight square.

"Honey, you are folding that napkin so tight," one of the men said.

"I know one thing: I don't have to fold anything together, but I sure as hell need to tuck," Edith said, and the men roared with laughter.

Cara smirked at that remark, grateful Edith was able to insert herself for Cara's sake. As they were talking about the SA and what Hitler was going to do for their country, Cara felt a tap behind her shoulder. When she turned around, she saw a woman with a short blonde bob and bangs, a flapper dress that looked oddly familiar and shiny, and she wore the reddest shade of lipstick Cara had ever seen.

"Can I help you?" Cara asked.

"You don't recognize me?" the woman asked.

Cara examined the woman again, looking at her up and down.

"Molly," she whispered.

"Who?" the woman asked.

Cara shook her head and realized it was their bartender.

Chapter 23

One of the SAs, Otto, asked Cara to sit on his lap. Cara, having nothing to lose, went over to Otto, as if floating, and sat. She was slightly intoxicated, and he was becoming more handsome with every drink. Cara had never done anything with a man before. She put her arms around Otto and brushed his blonde hair with her fingers.

"You know, I know you are concerned about an Aryan race, but there is nothing more attractive, in my opinion than a curly brunette," Otto remarked, "I think you'll be safe in the purge," he added with a wink.

"The purge?" she inquired.

"Well, to have an Aryan race, there has to be a purge of all other people with other features," he remarked.

Cara was careful. She could play this in one of two ways. "Well, thanks for keeping me safe, soldier," she added.

"You are stunning," he said.

"You are very handsome," she giggled, mimicking his every move.

"I have some money with me. Would you like it?" he asked in a whisper.

Cara paused and looked at her fingernails. "It depends on how much you have," she replied boldly.

"I have 100 □□ to do anything I want to you," he said.

She pondered this.

"If you had 150, I can do anything I want to *you*," she said with an evil grin.

"Shall we find a place to go then?"

She took him by the tie, led him upstairs to her former sewing room, and threw him on the bed. Cara was always curious about male anatomy, and outside of seeing Marie's flaccid penis, she had never really seen one fully erect. She took down the SA's trousers and saw an erect, perfectly pink knob wrapped up in a skin, something she hadn't seen before.

"You have been with a lot of Jewish guys?"

"Why do you ask?"

"A lot of Jews are circumcised. I'm not. I wasn't sure if you had seen one before. Anyway. Here it is 150 for the most beautiful woman I've ever seen."

"Well, I think that is the most beautiful penis I think I've ever seen," Cara remarked. She felt awkward. She wasn't quite sure what to do with it, but she knelt and touched it. It was soft and squishy. She grasped it a little firmer and started stroking it up and down. Otto seemed to like that and started moaning. She put it in her mouth and continued stroking, and Otto moaned louder. She decided to spit more on it; it was getting dry, and her spit seemed to lubricate the pocket.

"Stop, baby, stop. You're getting me all riled up. I want my money's worth," he said, ripping her last fine garment into two pieces.

She held back her emotion as the last bastion of who she used to be in Berlin fell to the ground. He flipped her onto her back and immediately entered her. Cara's body screamed in protest, but she commanded herself to let it happen. He had paid for this, after all. But it felt so unnatural. Eventually, she stared at the ceiling, willing it to be over.

Otto grunted a release. "Oh. I forgot a condom," he muttered and splayed out, sweating on her freshly cleaned sheets.

"That was amazing," she said in her best convincing voice. She nestled up to him and started making swirls in his chest hair. It felt like it was exfoliating her cheek.

"We can do that all the time soon enough," he said.

"What do you mean?"

"Well, we've bought this place from that red-haired man. The SA is going to take it over. We can make this our sex room," Otto said, lighting a cigarette.

"Oh, Ronan doesn't own this place. He's renting it." Her face turned red. She had figured she wasn't supposed to say that.

"Oh, then we probably bought it from the owner through him or something," he said. "Doesn't matter. This is a sex room, baby. Yes, our sex room. We'll be bringing in all the prostitutes before we get rid of them. More pleasure for us, doing the hard work."

"Get rid of them?" she asked curiously.

"Well, I'm probably not supposed to tell you this."

"If you tell me," Cara said and jumped on top of him, "I'll give you another ride," she giggled.

As the night trickled into the early morning, Cara favored taking a refilled bottle of bottom-shelf German whiskey up to her room to spend time with her own thoughts. The music from the club was still going strong, and sleep wouldn't catch her until daylight peeked through her curtains. She took swigs from the bottle and stared at the wall across from her room, with nothing on but her knickers. She noticed she was bleeding and still seeping out semen. She felt neutral and numb about

159

the entire process, but now, at least, she knew she could walk to a restaurant the next day and get a hot meal for her and Marie, which felt good.

* * *

Cara woke up the following day with a sense of dread. Until then, she had been reasonable about the closing of Eldorado, trusting Ronan in how he was going about everything. She was nervous now that he had accepted money when he shouldn't have, knowing she told the SA about him not owning the club outright. Cara rose from her bed, her skin clammy and pale, the stench of last night's party still on her clothes. Her head pounded in protest, and the fog of a hangover began to cloud her mind. She moved slowly, her hands shaking with every move. She found the bottle of whiskey from the night before and examined how much was left in it. It was about a quarter full, so she took a deep swig before stumbling over to put on a few items of clothing: an oversized fur coat and a pair of pajama trousers.

She stumbled out of her room and into the hallway, clutching the walls for support whenever she felt the room spinning. When she approached Ronan's door, she didn't knock. She walked in. She found him in bed, snuggled up with Edith. Edith was peacefully asleep on his chest, her head following the rising and falling of his breath. Edith hadn't taken off her eyelashes from the night before but had remembered to take off her wig. Ronan started to stir. He always was a light sleeper.

He squinted and rubbed his eyes with his free hand. He looked at Cara with furrowed brows.

"What are you wearing?" he laughed.

Although slurred, she spoke Irish to him for the first time since she had been there.

"Cad a bhfuil muid ag dul a dhéanamh?"

He sighed and sat up, gently moving Edith to the side. Edith flipped over on her own and went back to sleep. Ronan got out of bed and took Cara downstairs. He took out the small burner and started a pot of water for tea, and they started talking. He didn't say anything about Cara being intoxicated.

"I think I made a mistake, Ro," Cara said.

"What do you mean?" he asked.

"Well, I made some extra money yesterday with an SA, and he told me that the organization bought this place from you. And I let it slip that you weren't the owner, that it was probably someone else. We brushed it off; it was likely a miscommunication, but did you sell this place?"

The kettle started whistling, and Ronan poured two cups of boiling water into their ceramic mugs. He sighed and bowed his head for a moment.

"I planned to get the money and pay off the owners before they were none the wiser. The SA paid way more than this place is worth, and I figured I could pocket the difference without anyone knowing," he said.

"Ronan, that's fraud," Cara whispered.

"Isn't it fraud to be slowly priced out of a city we made? Isn't it fraud to go hungry to keep this club alive? Isn't it fraud to need to sell your body to live?"

Cara's face flushed.

He continued, "I can't live like this anymore. We can't live like this. Some big changes are coming to Berlin, Cara. And even if the SAs were to find out I'm not the legitimate owner, I know they wouldn't bat an eye. They want the same things we do, to live a normal life and not be out-priced by these elitist Jews."

"Whoa," Cara muttered.

"Look at what this state has done to us. All we do is drink and turn tricks. I can't even care for myself, let alone worry about you. I'm sorry, Cara. I think it's best if you are on your own for a while. I can't..." he started crying.

Cara held out her hand and put it on his arm. "Where are you going to go, Ronan? Do you not want me following you?" she asked, bleary-eyed.

He paused and wiped his face. "You need to get your life together without me," he sobbed, "I can't do this anymore. I'm sorry. I'm so sorry."

With her fur coat and trousers, she went into her sewing room for the last time. She gathered everything she owned and shoved them in her trunk, unsure of her plan. The room was still spinning, and she was reeling from the discussion. She realized she didn't have much as she packed, but she had money from the night before. She walked around the corner, in her mind, going to Marie's to figure out her plans. Even though Marie was a Nazi sympathizer, Cara at least knew she could count on her to help her figure things out.

Chapter 24

Father McKinny paced his office with his hands behind his back. Ronan sat in the hardwood chair and bit the edges of his nail bed, trimming off the dead skin with his teeth. Patrick was outside the office waiting to be called in separately.

"Tell me exactly what happened," Father McKinny said. "Wait, do not tell me what happened. I know what happened. Do you know that Father O'Malley took vows to be God's servant? That he is celibate?"

Ronan looked down at a hanging bit of skin on his finger before putting it into his mouth and biting it off.

"Ronan, you must say something," Father McKinny said.

Ronan rubbed his now bleeding finger on his trouser leg. "I don't want to talk about it," he muttered.

Father McKinny took an empty chair to Ronan and sat down. He put his hand on Ronan's. "Did he force this upon you?" Father McKinny asked seriously.

There was an out for Ronan if he wanted it. He chewed the inside of his cheek and avoided eye contact with Father McKinny, mulling over the question.

"I don't want to be punished," Ronan sobbed. "I did not want to do it, Father. He said it was God's wish and I was special for being chosen. I tried to leave this job so I did not have to see him any longer, but with Monsignor bringing me back and having no money, I had no other choice."

Father McKinny rubbed Ronan's back as he sobbed. "Would you like us to call the police and report him?"

"No, this is all so embarrassing, you must understand," Ronan cried.

Father McKinny took out a handkerchief and wiped his sweating forehead. His face was ashen, and he was muttering incomprehensible sounds that Ronan took for agreement. "We could deal with this matter quietly if that is your wish," Father McKinny said, looking at Ronan, hopeful he would agree.

"I want things to continue as they were. I want to go back to living a normal life. Except I do not wish to return to this job, and I have no money to sustain my family."

Father McKinny wrung his hands on his lap. "Perhaps the church volunteers could bring by shopping or help out with daily chores—"

"Volunteer help will not pay the rent, Father McKinny," Ronan said as he wiped his eyes.

Father McKinny rose from his seat and walked over to the desk. He pulled out a drawer and took out a modest stack of banknotes. "This was going to be Father O'Malley's one month's salary. I will give you my salary as well. However, how will I know you will not say anything before I do?" Father McKinny asked.

"You can trust me, Father McKinny," Ronan said.

"The reputation of St. Kevin's is on your shoulders. If I hear about this somewhere else, Ronan, I will deny it and blame you. I'll say you've been acting funny since your Da died, and you need a trip to the hospital to get straightened out. My word is gold against yours," he said.

Ronan stood up from his seat and held his palm out. Father McKinny handed him the banknotes.

"Pleasure doing business with you, Father," Ronan said, leaving the office.

He did not look at Father Patrick sitting on the chair outside. He walked out of St. Kevin's and never turned back.

* * *

Father McKinny did not need to worry about Ronan. When Father Patrick discovered that Ronan had blamed him for the incident, he marched over to the O'Shea household and demanded to speak with Ana, saying it was urgent. He told her that Ronan was poorly and that he had tried to touch Patrick intimately and then blamed him for it. Ronan said he would not say anything if he paid for his silence.

This struck Ana as strange. They had been living on what was left of his savings from his parish job. However, Ronan told Ana he did not have money to pay rent that month, as his savings had dwindled from supporting the family on his own. If it was confirmed that he had the money, he was not sharing it with his family. When Patrick left, Ana was in shock, pacing the floor of their one-bedroom flat and cursing Ronan's name. What would St. Kevin's think of the O'Shea family?

Ronan saw Father Patrick leave his block of flats as he was approaching, and his heart pounded in his chest. Although he was uncertain of what was said, he knew it would get him in immense trouble. Reading the writing on the wall, he ran to the Byrnne house. He remembered how Catherine had spoken of a more open-minded culture among her theater friends on

165

those afternoons when he visited the house.

Even though it was past eleven, Catherine opened the door, still wearing a nightgown. She invited him in, and he told her everything: the truth about the relationship that developed between him and Father Patrick, how he lied to get money, and how he now needed so desperately to flee before he was locked up in a hospital, his reputation wholly ruined.

Catherine passed along the name and address of a good friend, Edith Smith, an American in Berlin. Ronan left Catherine's, sent Edith a telegram, and booked the next train out of Dublin with a meager stack of banknotes and the clothes on his back.

Chapter 25

Marie made Cara a cup of tea when she appeared on her doorstep. Cara sobbed and told her about Ronan asking her to leave, saying that he couldn't take care of himself or another person.

Cara took the tea from Marie, put the cup to her lips, and drank. The warm liquid was comforting, but still, she yearned for something stronger. A glass of whiskey would ease her day's troubles even if it were watered down. Marie didn't have whiskey or liquor of any kind. All she had was tea and cheese, the latter growing a green film in her ice box. She would scrape off the bit of green and have the rest later, saying it was fine. It was like that.

Cara knew she couldn't live with Marie, could not live like Marie. Living with Marie meant supporting Marie financially, as Cara already paid for everything when they were together. Otherwise, she was convinced Marie wouldn't eat at all. If Jews were classified as the bourgeoisie in Berlin, then what the hell happened to Marie to have her live this way? She was barely scraping by, living on moldy cheese and handouts from the community.

It annoyed Cara in a way she could not explain. She loved Marie as a friend, and she had helped her through some tough times, but there was something about her always needing financial assistance. It was like she maintained a state of desperation so people would flock to her, wanting to help. Marie did have money to do whatever she wanted, but Cara often secretly questioned her impoverished state.

She took another sip of her tea and remembered to be grateful Marie had at least that to offer her. "I don't know what's happened to him," Cara sighed.

"For a foreigner, he surely feels entitled to a restored Germany," Marie retorted.

"He's been on edge lately. I made things worse for him. I think he's so stressed about what to do next with his life, and maybe this extremism is something he can hold onto, especially with his new SA friends," Cara said.

Marie poured more hot water into Cara's mug and made herself tea inside a measuring cup.

Cara sighed at this and shook her head behind Marie's back. "Marie. You can afford another mug," she chuckled.

"It's me by myself, dear. I only live on what I need," she answered, seemingly a canned response. She dipped the tea bag into the measuring cup.

Marie lifted her eyebrows, making wrinkles on her forehead. When she released the muscles, the wrinkles remained. Even her hands, once smooth and elastic, were starting to crepe, and now that her hair was longer and she no longer constantly wore her wig, Cara noticed how much gray was coming from her roots. She didn't know how old Marie was; she'd never asked. She placed her hand on Marie's.

"I don't know what to do. I can't go back to Ireland, but I can't stay here either, in Berlin. My sewing machine is sold. The club is closed. I had a horrible dream on Christmas when

168

I was sleeping on the park bench of people dying and being visited by Molly's dead mother. She told me to leave, to leave Germany. I can't describe it, but I have a desperate feeling I need to get out of here," Cara said.

Marie thought about this and scratched her chin, a small amount of stubble visible from not shaving the night before. "Why don't you go to America?"

"I don't know anyone there. I'd be on my own," Cara said. "What's happened to me, Marie? A little Catholic girl from Dublin, engaging in premarital homosexual sex, nudity, and prostitution."

"Sounds like a good time to me, honey," Marie said. "Here's what we're going to do. We'll plan your life tonight—a new life for Cara O'Shea, by Cara O'Shea. No one is going to make decisions for you anymore. What do you want?"

Cara paused at this question. "I feel like I got everything I wanted already. I got freedom, women, and a chance to be a well-known designer in this community. I had everything I could ever want, and now it's all gone. My Gran always said that God finds a way to punish sinners. He punished me for being with Molly and having her mom die. He's punishing me now. I've lost everything." Cara started to cry, "God, Marie. I really need a drink."

"How about some tea," Marie said, patting her hand. "God doesn't have to be the one you grew up with. There are so many interpretations of who and what a god is. My God is not a God of punishment. Molly's mom didn't die because you were in a relationship with Molly. You loved her. Love is powerful and pure; who is to say one kind of love is better? We're the closest of friends. I love you like my daughter, and I know you love me like a mother. We are a chosen family, and our bond

169

is not lessened by the fact we are not blood. The blood of the covenant is thicker than the water of the womb."

Cara sniffled.

"I've been around much longer than you have. I've come to find that my happiness is dependent on me. The more people I meet in this community, even worldwide, the more I understand what outsiders see as sinful. I see them as kids who never got to play in the sandbox together. We have power in numbers. These friendships I've had over the years mean more than any relationship I've ever had. They run deep. If you were to know God and what it truly means to you, wouldn't you think that God would want you to be happy? It's all made-up crap anyway, Cara. You know religion started as a cult; don't get me started on that," Marie said and lit a cigarette.

She blew out a puff of smoke. "My point is, create your own life. Whatever you believe to be true will be true. Now, darling. If your God was an ever-loving, accepting God who wanted what was best for you and loved you no matter what, what kind of life would you create for yourself? Let's close our eyes and envision!"

Cara closed her eyes and went inward. It felt strange to do this. She had never intentionally tapped into herself. She wasn't sure if she could trust what she would see, but she tried anyway.

She envisioned her life in a different country, in the countryside. She had a large house with a lot of land and saw a large dog with brown spots and a soft white chest. She saw her dining room table, filled with people she didn't recognize now but had a deep connection. They were all eating a dinner she had prepared, drinking wine, laughing, and loving on her. She saw herself in a room in the house, sketching outfits. Someone knocked on her door, entered with a hot cup of tea, and set it beside her. She looked up to see who had brought her this. She had dark brown hair in a chiffon, a fresh set of sunned freckles, and a button-down shirt tucked into a stylish pair of blue cropped trousers. She kissed her cheek and returned to the kitchen, dancing to something on the radio. Cara opened her eyes and discovered Marie's hand on hers. She had been crying.

"Now, as a little experiment, let's see what would happen if you stayed in Berlin.," Marie said.

Cara closed her eyes to tune into herself the same way she had before. She felt herself get pulled down to a dark place, and where she landed, she didn't see nearly the same scenario as she did when she envisioned her best life. Instead, she saw a massive trench from an aerial view. At first, it looked like fragments of something piled on one another, skinny, disembodied parts. As she got closer to the trench, it became much clearer what that something was. Dead bodies were strewn about in the trench, thrown in haphazardly, and piled on top of one another. They were all naked; they all looked starved, skin on bone, limbs entangled, and Cara couldn't differentiate one person from another. She estimated hundreds in that one area. She saw a shaved head of one of the bodies poking out in the pile, eyes popped open. Cara would recognize those eyes anywhere. It was Marie. Then, the vision turned visceral as she smelled the stench of hundreds of decaying bodies. She opened her eyes, ran to Marie's hallway toilet, and vomited all the contents of her stomach.

Marie came rushing down the hallway. "That's the tea, dear. It's cleansing," she said, coming to hold Cara's hair back. She had a tie, tied her hair up, and rubbed her back in the stall. "You may hallucinate with this tea," Marie said as she vomited. We can talk about this in the morning. Let's get you cleaned up. You're a mess."

Marie helped her into one of the shower stalls and turned on the water. However, water did not come out of the faucet; it was salt pellets. One hit Cara in the temple, and she passed out. She woke up, not to Marie standing over her, but Catherine. Except Catherine looked different. Her cheeks were sallow, her skin jaundiced, and she was clammy. She was completely naked. Her hair was wet and stringy, and she peered over Cara with concern.

"Catherine—"

"I told you to leave. You haven't left," she said, helping Cara sit up gently. Catherine sat down next to Cara and pulled her knees to her chest.

"I'm figuring it out," Cara said.

She turned to Cara and opened her mouth. A thick yellow gas was released from her mouth, and she began to transform. Her eyes went black, and her eyeballs and sockets grew into large ovals, taking over her face. Her teeth were sharp points. Her breasts shriveled up, her entire body almost melting away to skin and bone until Cara could see, to her horror, every single outline of bone beneath the skin, a mere outline of a skeleton.

Catherine crawled toward Cara, outstretching her right hand to touch Cara's hair, the cloud of gas getting thicker and thicker; Catherine was a demon coming to drag her to hell.

172

Chapter 26

When Cara came to, she was on the floor of Marie's flat in the fetal position. The right side of her face felt cold against the damaged wood floor. She had a good angle to see what was on Marie's floor: mostly dust, chipped pieces of finisher, and, in the corner, a few mouse droppings. Cara's stomach cramped and released, the release feeling like a wave of relief. She pushed herself up, her vision clouding as her body adjusted to the gravitational pull. The one-room flat was silent, and as she looked around, she saw Marie in her bed, reading a fashion magazine.

"How long was I out for?" Cara asked Marie.

Marie continued to flip through the magazine. "You've been here for a few days, love. In and out of consciousness," she said casually.

"A few days? That can't be right," Cara said. "Shouldn't I have gone to the hospital?"

"It's just mushrooms, dear. I've done this a few times. I have a client coming here in the afternoon, and I need you to leave. I'd ask you to join us; according to Edith, he pays very well, but you shouldn't have any relations in your state." Marie looked at her, "I'd recommend some fresh air and exercise. A brisk walk should make you feel much better. Then, come back here, and we'll discuss how you can help me pay rent! While you were sick, my landlord raised it by twenty percent. Who would have thought this little schwul ghetto would be priced so high?"

Cara turned from the floor and grabbed Marie's kitchen table to pull herself up. "What was in the cup of tea you made me?"

"Slowly, dear. Very slowly," Marie rushed over from her bed to help Cara. She almost collapsed in Marie's arms, but she was strong and was able to pull her into a chair.

"You need some food, Cara," said Marie, "and I'm afraid I don't have any. Hang on..." She got up and went into her covered drawer again. "Aha! I have chocolate." Her eyes brightened, "Always have chocolate on hand in case of emergencies. It's the biggest life lesson I can ever teach you," she said as she broke off a piece.

She put it down in front of Cara, who picked it up and inspected it, concerned.

"Oh, stop it; I know what you're thinking. I bought it in this century. In fact, I bought it last week," Marie said.

"Okay, good. Because I think the cheese in your ice box–"

"Was here when I moved in! Who doesn't love free cheese?" Marie said.

Cara scrunched her face. "Oh my God, Marie. That's–"

"I'm joking! It was worth it to see your face!" Marie laughed.

Cara bit into her piece of chocolate and felt warmth wash over her. She sighed in relief, and her hunger increased when she finished her chocolate. She stood up slowly and grabbed her coat. "I'm feeling hungry. Would you like to come with me to get something to eat before your lover boy shows up?"

"No thanks, love. I'm going to stay here. He'll be here in about thirty minutes, and I'll spend about an hour with him. Come back after that, and we'll continue talking about our future! I've had a few days to think about it, and I think a fresh start would be nice. What do you think about moving to America?" she asked.

"It sounds scary, but I would feel so much better if you were with me," Cara said. She approached Marie and hugged her tightly, "Thank you for taking care of me."

Marie hugged her back. "Now, get out of here," Marie said as she turned Cara around and patted her on the butt. "Us Jews aren't known for affection, but I love you, Cara O'Shea. You are my daughter."

Cara turned back around, "Marie! My momma!"

"Don't you dare come back here and hug me! I cannot ruin my makeup," Marie said.

Cara put her hands into the shape of a heart and peeked her eye through the open hole before turning away and opening the door to leave. A strange sensation washed over her, and she turned to look at Marie.

"Get out of here, you rascal!" Marie shouted.

Cara smiled and said, "I love you too, Mom," leaving Marie in her silk pink robe, which she had made from an old costume from Eldorado and one of her best blonde wigs.

Cara tried to waste as much time as possible before returning to the flat. She remembered reading much about New York in her fashion magazines, that it was the next up-and-coming fashion capital. She figured she could enter the fashion spotlight similarly to how she did in Berlin. She went for lunch and walked around the block a few times before stopping in a grocery store to pick up more chocolate, wine, and cheese. She headed back to Marie's around four hours later, even though she said she only needed two, just in case her client appointment ran over late. She knocked on the front door, but

175

Marie did not come. She eventually let herself in but didn't see Marie. It was quiet in the room.

"Marie?" she called out, "Marie? Where are you?"

What Cara saw next would haunt her for the rest of her life. Marie was in her bed, covered in blood. Her eyes were wide open, and so was her mouth. Cara screamed and ran to the hallway telephone to call for help.

Chapter 27

Cara had walked around Marie's block so many times that holes were forming in the soles of her shoes. The Kerry green coat she had arrived with in Berlin was tattered and had large holes. Whenever she went to put it on, another layer would rip, as if the fabric itself was disintegrating with every touch. There was no use in mending something that was further rotting with wear, but she wore it anyway and braced herself against the January chill. Her face had spots of dirt caked on it, and though she was living in Marie's flat without Marie and religiously checked her pocket every morning to ensure she still had cash to flee, she couldn't bring herself to do what she needed to, so she paced around the block. She patched the soles of her shoes up with glue and discarded cardboard she found in a dumpster. Though she witnessed the aftermath of Marie's murder, there were no tears that streaked her face, instead a blank, empty stare as she paced the block, occasionally allowing her eyes to blink against the harsh wind.

There was no funeral for Marie, and no matter how hard Cara investigated, it didn't seem like she had any family to contact. The burial was immediate, and Cara signed over Marie's body to the state, though it was not her body to sign over. She did not hire professional cleaners to clean up the mess that was all over the flat. Instead, she had purchased strong cleaning products the police recommended and got to work, rewetting the dried blood on the wood floor, the stench of it attracting creatures that came out of the woodwork. The wood absorbed the blood stain, and the landlord had promised Cara he would fix it, but weeks had gone by and every morning Cara looked over at the spot, the only physical connection remaining to Marie.

There was no investigation due to the nature of Marie's death. There was no support for a crossdressing prostitute who was murdered. After all, the police had said, this was the cost of sexual immorality, and Cara was once again reminded that both the law and religion were tied together. God was disappointed in Cara, she was sure of it. She had lost every ounce of innocence and came a long way from stealing communion wine and corrupting her best friend. The memories of Molly were all that got her through these times. Looking back, they seemed so innocent when they were hiding and kissing and rolling around in the grass. When day would fade into night, the stars would illuminate the sky and all there was in the world was the magic of them and their youth. Where would she go from here? The memories themselves were almost as painful as living in her present.

Cara had gone to tell Ronan of Marie's death but could not find him. Instead, covering the former club was a large red flag, a white circle, and the symbol of the rise to power, a swastika covering the entire building. Hitler was officially in power, and according to the news circulating, all unnatural sexual tendencies were officially outlawed. There was a return to moral upstanding. Magnus was said to be in hiding, though Cara had tried to get in contact with him to no avail.

According to a few of the former Eldorado workers, Ronan had moved to the countryside and joined the SA. He ditched Edith, and no one had heard from her since. Slowly, without anyone realizing what was happening, Cara's community had disintegrated after the closing of the club. Everyone she had tried to hold onto was slipping through her fingers like sand. She hadn't eaten in days, and whenever she would pass by a building with a reflection, all she saw was a walking skeleton with skin. She still dreamed of Catherine but started to make demands of her, pleading with her to take her soon, anything to end the numbness she felt all over her body and to dive into the relief of death. She yearned desperately to fall asleep and never wake up again.

It had become Cara's responsibility to go through the items Marie had left behind in her efficiency flat, though by the looks of it, there likely wouldn't be much to go through. The tricky part about Marie was, though, the hidden elements of her life. She could hide an entire herbal remedy drawer, and no one would be the wiser. So, Cara got to work, sorting through drawers, lifting the bottoms of dividers, and discovered a world of treasures under the perceived scarcity. Underneath a divider in one of the drawers, Bakelite bracelets and necklaces were thrown together in one large, tangled mess. The vibrant pearl pinks, reds, and rich dark greens were threatening Cara's gray composure. Yet, she felt drawn to pick up a piece Marie wore frequently, with a long silver chain and small shiny crimson Bakelite beads. She undid the clasp and pulled the chain around her neck and bushy hair. She clasped it in the back, and when she pulled her hair out of the chain, clumps of it began to come out in her hand. It had been weeks since Cara could do anything but go through the motions. However, at that

179

moment she started to sob, with big belly cries, and a heaving chest. She backed up to the wall behind her, slid down, her knees to her chest, and let everything go.

She half expected someone to come and check on her in this state. Yet no one did. She was alone, living on memories to avoid the present. When her deep cries faded into gulps of air and sniffles, she looked more closely at the necklace, fingering the thick beads between her fingers before chucking them across the room and folding her arms across her chest. She felt each individual rib on the side of her body poking through her skin. She sat like that with her back against the wall for some time, staring at nothing in particular, completely spacing out. How different her life was only a few years ago, posing for *Die Freundin*, the newspaper that was not on the newsstands anymore. In Marie's ghetto, not too long ago, the Jewish businesses were being boycotted and looted. There was no government discouragement of this, and all Cara did was watch it all happen.

It was like everything was happening in slow motion. One thing happening after another, without a way to pause and reflect on any one tragedy.

After she paused in her sadness, Cara decided to try and go through Marie's belongings again. She found a bag of white powder; she assumed it was cocaine that was left over from her floor days. Cara decided to partake, even though it was only ever something she did if she had a very late night with costumes at Eldorado. It gave her energy she had not had in a while, and with the extra jolt, she decided to go to Marie's bathroom to wash herself. Cara had not had a scrubbing since Marie had given her the tea, approximately three weeks ago. She scrubbed every orifice. She then put on a freshly laundered dress, one that was too big for her, but she would wear one of Marie's coats over it so no one would notice. She had some leftover hair paste from Edith that she put through her hair to make her curls soft and supple. When she looked at herself in the mirror, she looked like she had before her life had begun to go awry. She counted up her money and counted Marie's stash too that she had left behind. In total, she had the equivalent of 3,000 US dollars stashed away. She pocketed the money and decided today would be the day to go to Cook's for Travel Agency. She would book a ticket to the United States. She didn't know if it was the hit of cocaine or the sheer state of being left with absolutely nothing to keep her company except Marie's blood stain, but she felt it was time to get herself out of Germany and start life on her own terms like Marie would have wanted.

Cara hadn't thought much about her present, it was too painful day after day to sit with the unknown of what she was to do, with no one to rely on but herself, and to think of the responses from loved ones who had either removed themselves from her life by death or by direct purpose of separation. She didn't understand why people feared abandonment. There was a comfort to being by herself that she couldn't quite explain, though it wasn't in her best interest to be alone, as she wasn't taking the greatest care of herself. This could be seen by the shelf of empty liquor and wine bottles lining Marie's windowsills, doing cocaine in the middle of the day on a bright and sunny Saturday. She did not know another way to survive it. She did hear the United States had banned liquor. Maybe she could survive there knowing there would be no liquor for her to drink even if she wanted to. She tried to think of all the places she wanted to live, and although New York sounded

181

appealing, Chicago seemed like the perfect fit. It was like a little Berlin, and of all her friends who traveled, they said that Chicago had the best underground scene. You had to know where to look.

She ensured there were no rips, tears, or pieces of lint on her clothing. She put on a pair of shoes where the cardboard wasn't missing and marched down to the office. However, when she saw her reflection in the Cook's window, she thought it quite yellow and pallid. She quickly powdered her nose using the window as a mirror, and ensured that what was left of her dark curls shone brightly.

The office itself was nothing spectacular. A man greeted her with a thick mustache and gold wire-rimmed glasses. He looked to be around forty and when Cara walked in, he was staring off into space, a thin stack of papers next to him. It was as if Cara interrupted a dream he was having, and he was at first disturbed by her appearance. Then, as he realized that she was, indeed, a customer, he moved his few papers around and asked her to sit on his polished wooden chair opposite him. The pits of his white button up shirt were yellowed, and dark brown circled around his collar. The man did not appear to be sweating, but the evidence suggested that at one time he did profusely. Cara fidgeted with the elastic end of her coat.

"I'm looking to book midline travel accommodations to the United States," she said, her voice cracking. The man eyed her.

"Who will be accompanying you?" he asked.

"Well, my sister," she trailed off.

"No man to accompany you on this trip?" he interrogated.

"I'm sorry, sir. My sister is deceased. Her funeral is going to be held in New York, and I was hoping to get accommodations for myself to be there in time for the funeral. They are pausing everything while the family comes in. I do not have a husband yet, but I do have the money required to book a cabin on an ocean liner if you'll accommodate me," she said as eloquently as possible.

"That will cost you up to three thousand Reichsmarks, depending on what kind of cabin you want to stay in, young lady," he said. He began playing with his mustache and twirling the thick bristly hair between his index finger and thumb.

"I am aware of that. Please let me know what my options are," she asked, thumbing through the money she had in her pocketbook.

"You would need to pay at least half the amount today," he continued.

"I am prepared for that," she insisted.

He showed her a map of the different routes the ocean liners voyaged. The map was beautifully outlined, the vibrant colors of the countries popping out in deep hues of blue, purple, and burgundy. She thumbed over a route that went from a port out of Hamburg with Hamburg Amerika.

"How would I get to Hamburg?" she asked.

"By train, of course. I can set that ticket up for you as well. When were you looking to—"

"I'm looking to book as soon as possible. I need to be there for my family," she insisted.

He looked at the various departure dates on the Hamburg Amerika schedule.

"There is a boat leaving in two days to New York out of Hamburg. The journey will take you a week," he said. He began to fill out a travel document for her, writing down her name and circling her destinations.

"This is a newer boat called the Canard. It is fast and efficient and will get you to your destination quickly. What is your nationality?"

"Irish," she replied.

"You're lucky. You will not need a visa," he said. "Now, let's talk cabins."

Cara chose the most economical single-person cabin with shared toilet accommodations. She would need the rest of her money to get back on her feet and figure out a way to stay under the radar in the United States. As the man kept talking to her about different options and the type of food served on board, she could hear him, but she wasn't listening. It was as if everything that was happening was surreal, that she was not of this world, that this wasn't actually happening. Was she really fleeing? There was no reason to stay in a place that no longer supported her. She no longer belonged in Dublin. She no longer belonged in Berlin. She could make a new life for herself on her own terms. The community that had welcomed her with open arms had disbanded. She was alone. Marie was dead. She was haunting her both in the waning days with her visible blood stain on the hardwood floor of the efficiency flat and in her nightmares where she sat with her, listening to her reminisce about how they had it so good before the club closed. The life she was thrust into, she felt so lucky to experience, because she knew that this life could not exist anywhere else. She was sure of it. Even going back to the United States, she had read that the US was still in hiding their sexuality in the dark. That police were knocking down doors of suspected homosexuals and arresting them on uncertain terms. She was frightened by this possibility of being discovered, but it was better than the fear she had of staying in Berlin. The fear she had not knowing if she could survive another day or if she too would be murdered and not investigated. She was disposable. No one had any idea where she was, nor did they care. And in the face of this reality, Cara had to make a choice to either lay down and die or survive. And whatever was left of her instincts had told her survival was the choice to make.

Epilogue

Cara's journey on the Canard was nothing special. Her accommodations were modest, but she had three meals per day and mostly kept to herself. She had spoken with a few Americans during mealtimes and asked if they knew of any Irish communities in America. Almost every passenger she interviewed mentioned Chicago having one of the largest Irish populations. After disembarking in New York, she booked a train ticket from New York to Chicago.

She arrived in Chicago on February 14th, in nothing but a trench coat and reinforced shoes. That damned wind found its way through every pinhole in her coat and took her breath away. She had a small amount of money left and used it to stay in a modest motel on the city's South side.

From what she could drag out of the train conductor in attempted small talk, this part of the city had established Irish immigrants in a neighborhood called Bridgeport. Cara decided to chat up the motel owner to see if he knew of anyone looking for work, and he informed her of the booming industry in the neighborhood, how the retail factory was searching for seamstresses, preferably those with prior experience with sewing machines.

The first day she went to inquire about the job, she met a

woman at the front desk with dark brown hair in a chiffon, stunning blue eyes, and a collared blouse with only three top buttons. She introduced herself as Gwyn and had an accent Cara could not pinpoint immediately.

"My name is Cara. John, the owner of Bridgeport Motel, said you were searching for someone with sewing experience. I'm here to apply for the position," she said.

Gwyn squinted for a moment. "Are you from Ireland?" she asked.

Cara's red lips stretched into a smile. "I am. I know you are not from America, but I cannot place your accent."

"It is a difficult accent to understand. I'm from Wales, a small town called Llangollen," she replied.

Cara smiled. "I have never been to Llangollen, but I have heard a lot about its infamous ladies."

Gwyn's face flushed and she laughed. She asked Cara to follow her to the manager's office. And, after Cara interviewed for the job, Gwyn asked Cara to join her for a cup of coffee.

About the Author

Caitlin is the author of *Beyond a World Apart*. She is passionate about uncovering LGBTQ history and telling queer stories. Caitlin is a student at the Writer's Studio and lives in Tucson, Arizona with her girlfriend and two pups.

You can connect with me on:
🌐 https://www.cemwrites.com

Subscribe to my newsletter:
✉ https://caitlinemyers.substack.com